PRAIRIE HEARTS

PRIMROSE SERIES
BOOK FOUR

TANYA RENEE

To those that serve, my deepest respect and to those that wait patiently, you are my heroes.

ALSO BY TANYA RENEE

Primrose Series

Prairie Sky

Prairie Nights

Prairie Fire

Prairie Hearts

Prairie Sound

PROLOGUE

$\mathcal{I}$t was a beautiful prairie night. A million stars blanketed the sky, sparkling radiantly above. A night full of promises and dreams. The kind of night that made you feel like anything was possible. Prairie Sound was playing a set of sultry ballads, and the dance floor was full of couples and lovers swaying rhythmically to the music.

It was late and Garrett and Bea's wedding was winding down for the night. The happy couple, already whisked away by a limo for their wedding night.

Marnie Perez was picking at her second piece of wedding cake, a lemon chiffon creation she made special for the couple. As she enjoyed the decadent confection, she tried, rather unsuccessfully, to temper her awareness of the sexy man sitting next to her at the head table. Davis Baxter, the brother of the bride, the object of her affection and all her wildest fantasies. He was intense, broody, flirtatious, and she knew he had the ability to make her melt in his presence. Perhaps it was how unconventionally handsome he was with his short military cut, fiery red hair, piercing green eyes and his strong clefted jawline. Perhaps it was the vision of him in his military uniform the day they met that was permanently burned on her brain. Perhaps it was all the time they spent together leading to their first incredible kiss and the night they almost… Maybe it was a combination of everything that made him so perfect in her eyes. He could make her knees weak with the smallest of glances, and she was smitten. Unquestionably, she had it bad.

Having been put into a position of living together for two intense weeks just a year and a half ago, she was very aware of his eyes, always watching her. How he would follow her movement around the house, like a tiger tracking prey. Yet, she didn't feel like a helpless little animal waiting to be gobbled up. She felt sexy, womanly, and desired. Seeing him today had been sweet torture as she tried to resist giving into his advances and her own almost uncontrollable urges. Every opportunity he had today, leading up to this moment, he had made it abundantly clear that he still wanted her, and right now, sitting next to him, her resolve was cracking at a rapid pace.

"Do you want to dance?" he asked, leaning into her, and putting his hand on her thigh, his touch like a brand searing through her dress. Her body instantly heated from his proximity. The smell of his spicy cologne, intoxicating.

Marnie met his mesmerizing emerald eyes and, instantly entranced, she nodded, feeling her willpower holding on by a mere thread as he took her hand and led her around the table to the dance floor. A swoony power ballad sounded from the band, and he pulled her into him, his large hand gripping her waist and his muscular arms enveloping her. Her chest pressed to his hard muscular form; her mind swirled, consumed by her overwhelming lust for this man as she self-indulgently inhaled his masculine scent. *Oh God, he smells so good.* Her internal thoughts waging war with her heart as she swallowed nervously. *I can't give in. Oh, how I want to give in.*

His intense gaze bore into her, shadowed with desire, and her pulse spiked, her heart beating wildly in her chest as he leaned into her, his deliciously rough stubbled cheek brushing against hers. His hot breath, like feathers tickling her face, as he asked, "Do you want to get out of here?"

arnie Perez loved the quiet of her bakery early in the morning. 5 a.m. was the perfect time of day in her books. It was so peaceful and sometimes she would just take a moment to enjoy the tranquility of the quiet before the rush of the day. Since opening Everything you Knead, her beloved bakery, almost two years ago, she still couldn't believe she was 26 and a successful business owner. It wasn't surprising, knowing her family. Coming from a big Mexican family, her Abuela owned a successful Mexican restaurant in St. Augustine, The Blue Corn and her Padre and Madre owned a print company making marketing materials for local businesses. Being the only girl amongst four boys, most were entrepreneurs or aspiring entrepreneurs with a few creatives in the mix, like her brother Ramiro, who was riding the waves of success with his band, Prairie Sound. Without question, the Perez family were hard workers, and that work ethic was born and bred into each and every one of them.

A huge part of the success of her business was because of the wonderful community of Primrose. This southeastern Manitoba community opened their arms to her first when she started baking for the Eazy Café, the local greasy spoon and meeting place for everyone in town, and now with her own business. Marnie felt blessed to be a part of this community and quickly fell in love with the quaint simplicity of Primrose.

Setting out all her ingredients for her regular morning baking routine, she started the task of first making bread and pastries, then on to cupcakes and muffins and lastly the cookies. After that, she would spend her time on cakes and later in the day was reserved for custom orders. With her plan in place, she lifted a large bag of flour off the ground and started pouring it into the industrial mixer. Suddenly feeling lightheaded and dizzy, she wobbled slightly. Dropping the now half-empty bag to the floor, she grabbed onto the counter trying to steady herself, needing to get her bearings. *That was weird.* Taking in some deep cleansing breaths and reaching for the bag of flour again. As she did, an overwhelming wave of nausea overtook her. Dropping the bag again, she cupped her hand over her mouth, knowing that she needed to run to reach the bathroom on time. Barely making it to the toilet, she dropped to her knees, her body retching and stomach roiling, her breakfast emptying into the bowl. Marnie sat back on her heels, groaning, taking a moment to steady herself. Finally, feeling like it was safe to stand, she awkwardly got to her feet and leaned over the counter for a moment, taking in deep cleansing breaths to calm her stomach and her now aching head. Glancing up at her reflection, she wiped away the mascara that ran from under her eyes. *I can't afford to get sick. Far too much work to do.* Taking a paper towel, she wet it with cold water and put it against her cheek, dabbing one side and then the other. Setting her palm on her forehead to check for the familiar heat of a fever, she frowned. *Nothing. Strange.* She seldom threw up, even when sick, and prided herself on having an iron stomach. Perhaps she was coming down with something or perhaps... a passing thought went through her mind and she gulped as realization struck. *Oh no.*

* * *

A YEAR AND A HALF AGO – **5 days before Christmas**

Marnie watched as her housemate Bea Baxter bounded off her porch with excitement to greet the truck that pulled into their driveway. She swallowed down hard, feeling a little nervous about meeting Bea's younger brother Davis. Since she was renting a room in the home that they co-owned, she felt a little like an unwelcome guest at this moment. Putting those feelings aside and with Bea's reassurance, she decided she could handle sharing a home with someone she didn't know. Besides, she was swamped at the bakery and would likely be preoccupied. With it being Christmas week, she would be working overtime to fill last-minute Christmas orders and in between she would partake in the Perez Navidad traditions. Their paths would seldom cross during the next two weeks, so sharing a home was no big deal. At least that was what she kept telling herself.

Bea squealed, breaking her thoughts and bringing her back to the present. She watched as the truck door opened and a man wearing a military uniform and blue beret stepped out. Before she could get a good look at him, Bea tackled the man standing in their driveway. A deep rich laugh echoed in the cold crisp winter air, but with the sun newly set and only the porch light on, it was hard to make out her temporary housemate's face. She squinted as Bea and her brother approached and climbed the stairs towards her and Bea's boyfriend, Garrett, the sound of his combat boots heavy on the wood surface. Marnie's breath caught as Davis Baxter came into view, a large duffle bag slung over his broad shoulders, and her eyes met the most mesmerizing emerald, green eyes she had ever seen. His gaze drifted over to her, and Garrett then flitted back to her, and Marnie was transfixed as a slow smile curled his lips. Instantly butterflies took flight in her belly, the sensation surprising her.

"Let's all go inside, get you settled, and I will make introductions." Bea said happily as she opened the front door, leading Davis, Garrett, and Marnie into the house.

"Not much has changed. The house still looks like "Nanners", Davis's rich deep voice said as Bea led him down the hallway to the bedrooms.

Marnie shuffled into the kitchen with Garrett, who glanced down at her and smiled, looking as eager as she was to finally meet Davis. As they waited for Bea and Davis to emerge from the hallway, doors opened and closed, and a combined laughter echoed through the house. Coming around the corner, Marnie could finally get her first good look at the man she was about to share a home with. Davis Baxter stood around 6 feet tall, was bulky in build with broad shoulders, thick muscular arms, a cinched waist and narrow hips. His powerful and strong physique was perfectly matched by his thick neck and strong square jawline. But what was most striking about him were his amazing green eyes and the fiery red stubble that adorned his chin with a small cleft. It made him look wild and burly, and Marnie had never seen a man quite like him. Davis was, without a doubt, extremely attractive. Removing his beret, exposing his shortcut, red hair the same shade as Bea's, Davis smiled at both Garrett and Marnie, his gaze lingering on her.

Putting out his hand to Garrett, Bea made introductions. "Davis, this is Garrett Smithfield, my boyfriend. His daughter, Amelia, isn't here tonight, but you'll meet her tomorrow."

The men shook hands in greeting, "Nice to meet you." Davis said, then turning his gaze to Marnie, his eyes flashed playfully at her, as a small smile tugged at his lips and he asked. "You must be Marnie, my housemate for the next two weeks?"

Marnie could feel a blush rise on her cheeks, but her eyes couldn't break from his penetrating gaze as she answered nervously and put her hand out to him, "I am. Marnie Perez, pleasure to meet you."

Davis took her hand in his, a jolt of electricity crackling between them as he mumbled in reply, his words barely audible, "The pleasure is all mine."

Bea, seeming to pick up on the attraction, interrupted the moment. "Well, then…Marnie is kind of the housemate extraordinaire. She owns a bakery on Main Street, and I'm sure you'll have your fill of her confections in your two weeks here." Bea added, giving Marnie a playful smile, followed by a discerning wink.

"I work long hours too, so I shouldn't be in your way too much." Marnie blurted out, still feeling the heat in her face and internally groaning at how awkward she was being.

Davis's eyes brazenly surveyed her head to toe, lifting back up to meet her gaze before commenting. "We'll figure it out."

"Okay then!" Bea exclaimed, curious brows raised, interrupting the tension filled moment. "Garret and I will be across the street, if you need us, and will you come over for breakfast tomorrow morning?" she asked, turning to face Davis. "You can meet Amelia and since I got time off work for your entire stay, I want to spend as much time together as we can before you go back."

Davis nodded, offered his sister a smile, and pulled her in for a side hug. Shaking Garrett's hand again as Marnie watched them make their way to the door. "See you guys tomorrow." Davis said as she heard the door close and let out a nervous breath. *You got this Marnie.*

DAVIS CLOSED his eyes and let out a long exhale as he stood with his hand still on the front door. *Home.* He was home, but not alone. The most beautiful woman he had ever laid eyes on was waiting for him in the kitchen and standing here too long attempting to collect himself would come across as strange. *Dude, pull yourself together.*

He swallowed down hard, trying to steady his rapidly beating heart. *Be cool.* Taking off his uniform jacket, he hung it up on a front entrance hook and made his way into the kitchen, trying to act nonchalant and unaffected by his stunning housemate.

Marnie had her head in the refrigerator and was pulling out some containers as well as what looked like a covered cake holder. "Are you hungry?" she asked, glancing back at him, flashing him a sweet smile.

"Ah, sure, what do you got there?" he asked, taking a seat at the peninsula on a kitchen stool, and leaning in to peek into the containers she was opening.

"Tamales and carnitas tacos." she answered, rolling her the 'r' in carnitas a hint of her Spanish accent coming out. *That's so damn sexy.* "Do you like Mexican food?"

"I love it," he replied, his eyes taking in the amazing spread. "Don't tell me you made all of this."

Marnie smiled; her soft brown eyes sparkling with delight at his comment. "I can cook, but I can't take credit. My Abuela made all of this. She owns a Mexican Restaurant in St. Augustine."

"So, entrepreneurship is in your blood?" he asked as he watched her pull two plates out of the cupboard, start filling each plate with a little from each container and put the first plate into the microwave to heat it up.

"I guess you could say that," she replied, finishing her preparations by spooning out bowls of fresh salsa and guacamole. "My parents have their own business as well."

"Interesting." he said as she retrieved the first plate and set it in front of him. Looking at the feast before him, he inhaled deeply the savory spices perking his senses and making his mouth water. "This all looks amazing."

Marnie offered him another smile, retrieving her heated plate and rounded the counter, taking a seat on the stool next to him. The awareness of her proximity making his heart jump and body awaken from the alluring woman at his side. Marnie Perez was everything he was attracted to. She was petite, maybe around five foot five, soft and curvy in all the right places, a voluptuous hourglass figure that made him want to coast his hands over the shape of her. He liked a woman he could hold on to and he was very aware of how amazing it would feel to hold onto her. And then there was her gorgeous face. Lush, pillowy lips that begged to be kissed, high cheekbones that he wanted to trace with his fingertips and the most gorgeous chocolate brown eyes, so large and expressive. He had never seen eyes quite that color. Like hot chocolate. They were stunning.

"Dig in." she said, gesturing to the homemade tortillas.

Eagerly he helped himself to one and made himself a carnitas taco, dressing it with fresh salsa and guacamole. Taking his first bite, he groaned, a low guttural groan he knew may have sounded obscene, but he didn't care. *They definitely don't serve food like this on the base.* Then he lifted a bite of the tamale to his mouth, savoring the spicy sweet corn flavor. "Wow, these are amazing," he said, looking at his plate and then to Marnie.

"They're my Abuela's specialty." she replied proudly, taking a bite of hers.

"Honestly, this may be the most delicious Mexican

food I have ever had," he said, taking another bite and nodding his head with satisfaction.

Marnie smiled, got up from her seat and rounded the counter, headed for the fridge. "Beer?" she asked, glancing over her shoulder, her perfectly arched eyebrow raised.

I need to fucking marry this woman! "Sure." he replied, reaching over to grab the beer from her hand, his fingertips brushing hers. Their eyes met, a pulsing heat passing between them. The touch was so small, but intense. "Thank you."

Nervously, she broke their eye contact, grabbed one for herself and went back to her seat. *She felt that too.* As they ate together in relative silence, he could feel her heat next to him suddenly, very aware of how long it had been since he'd been with a woman. *Too damn long.*

Breaking the awkward silence, Davis turned his gaze to Marnie. "Thank you for this. Seriously, I haven't eaten this good in a while and I think I'm going to enjoy living with you for the next two weeks."

Marnie met his gaze, her eyes brightening with his gratitude. Awkwardness eased between them; they chatted lightly as they continued to eat. Davis asked her questions about her business and her family, and with each question he asked, Marnie volleyed back with questions for him. He was generally a guarded person, and seldom shared things about himself, preferring to be the inquisitor rather than the subject. Marnie matched him, and the conversation flowed easily and abundantly between them. Soon the plates had been emptied with both enjoying not just the food but the company.

"I don't think I could eat another bite," he said, patting his trim stomach.

"So, I assume you don't have room for this?" Marnie asked, lifting the cover on the cake holder revealing a decadent chocolate Bundt cake.

Davis's eyes widened, and he squinted at her, remarking, "Devil woman. Chocolate is my kryptonite."

"It's Mexican Chocolate, so it has a hint of cayenne. It's my favorite." She shared with a smile as she retrieved two small plates and cut him a big slice.

"A little spicy like you?" he asked flirtatiously, offering her a mischievous grin.

"As a matter of fact, yes, it is," she replied, her cheeks taking on a rosy hue as she cut herself a piece. Marnie paused, her fork poised as her gaze settled on him, watching as he cut a piece with his fork and brought the first bite to his mouth. The rich chocolate flavor rolled over his tongue, leaving it tingling from the heat of the cayenne. His eyes rolled back in approval, and Marnie giggled, a sweet melodic sound he instantly wanted to hear so much more of.

They ate their cake together, conversation continuing to flow as he watched her clean up, insisting that he sit back and relax after his long journey home. Marnie moved around the kitchen with grace, everything fluid and effortless. Davis was transfixed. He had only known this beautiful Latina for an hour, and he could already feel the sweet quell of desire building inside him. *Seriously Davis, get yourself together. Remember, you leave in two weeks.* Marnie turned, catching his stare and she flashed him her gorgeous smile, causing his heart to flutter wildly in his chest. *I'm in so much trouble.*

CHAPTER 2

$\mathcal{M}$arnie was born knowing family was the center of her universe and thanks to her religious Abuela, she grew up understanding the wrath of God. As she sat there, staring down at the positive pregnancy test in her hands, she was certain she was going to hell. *What am I going to do? She* asked herself, staring at the two pink lines in disbelief. *A baby, surely my family will be happy. It's not like I'm 16 or anything. I'm 26 and a grown ass woman.* She tried to reason, her mind reeling. *But I'm also 26 years old, and I know better. Why didn't we use protection?*

Marnie's thoughts drifted to that fateful night, the night she slept with Davis Baxter. The night they left together after Bea's wedding four weeks ago. How they barely made it into the house before his lips crashed with hers in a mind melding kiss, as he pressed her into the wall with his hard, heavy body, the feel of his arousal making her body beg for more. How they frantically shed their clothes, their eyes locked on each other as they fell together to the bed, his hard powerful body covering hers as he kissed her senselessly. How large rough hands roamed over her ample curves, touching all the places she craved him, eliciting moans and cries of pleasure. How he slowly sank into her, his eyes not leaving hers, the feel of him filling her painful at first, then morphing into something exquisite as he ground his body into her with sweet friction. His dirty words, telling her how good she felt, how sexy she was, and how her skin tasted like sugar. Their connection was explosive, almost primal as he took her again and again, making her detonate with pleasure.

Marnie touched her face, now flushed hot as her heart hammered in her chest, remembering every detail of that memorable night. The night she gave her virginity to the man she had desired for so long. She shook her head, trying to shake the memories from her consciousness, and stared down at the pregnancy test in her hands. Her life was on track, she had a successful business, amazing friends and was just at the beginning of her independent adult life. And now she was going to be a mother. Setting the test down on the bathroom counter, she buried her head in her hands and let the emotion wash over her as she cried.

* * *

A YEAR AND A HALF AGO, **4 days before Christmas**

Marnie woke the next morning with a start. Being a morning person, she never minded the early mornings of a baker. She always found the solitude grounding and loved that time of day when no one was around. Jumping out of bed with a start, she opened her bedroom door and padded down the hallway to the bathroom to get ready for her day. Showered, hair dried and makeup done, she wrapped her robe around her and made her way back to her bedroom to get dressed. It was Tuesday and four days till Christmas, so with her long to-do list running through her head, she slipped into a comfortable pair of jeans and a long sleeve red t-shirt that said. "Everything you Knead" on the front. Putting on her favorite pair of red Chucks, she pulled her shoulder length wavy hair back at the sides and took a long look at her reflection in the mirror. She liked what she saw and smiled. She had always been a little curvier than most, and what made her insecure in her teen years, now was something she loved about her body. She had curves for days, an hourglass figure and if not having those curves meant she had to give up cake, she was not about to make that sacrifice.

Making her way out of her room, she heard the clang of pans in the kitchen and her brows drew together. *Was Davis up already?* Slowly she rounded the case opening to find Davis, her sexy as hell housemate, in a pair of slim workout pants, and a white t-shirt that stretched over his muscular upper body. Between his shoulder blades was a line of sweat soaking through the shirt and his face was red and flushed from exertion. He looked like he'd just completed an intense workout, and Marnie internally groaned at the tantalizing sight of him. *He is so yummy.*

"Good morning." she said brightly, trying to mask her attraction to the man occupying the kitchen.

Davis turned, the sexy red stubble on his chin a little longer than the night before making him look sort of rugged and edgy. He flashed her his gorgeous smile and replied, "Good morning. Would you like some eggs?"

Surprised, Marnie sat down at the counter, a smile tugging at her lips as she nodded and watched as he cracked some eggs into an already heated pan and put bread into the toaster. "Why are you up so early?" she asked, as he turned and put a steaming mug of coffee in front of her.

"I'm an early riser too, so I went for a run and figured I would fix you some breakfast before you go into work," he said, glancing over his shoulder. "You drink coffee, right?"

"I do," she said, cupping the warm mug in her hands and breathing deeply the rich smell before she lifted it to her lips. Letting the strong bitterness soothe her, she let out a long sigh.

Davis turned, his gaze roaming over her. "You look pretty today," he said. "I like the red."

Marnie's hand smoothed over her shirt, his compliment making her stomach do a somersault. She wasn't used to compliments, especially from a sinfully handsome man that was making her breakfast.

"Thank you." she said, offering him a sweet smile. He turned the frying pan in hand and slid two fried eggs on her plate, then added two pieces of hot buttered toast.

"This looks delicious." She commented, taking in her plate of food and meeting his gaze.

"It's the least I could do after you fed me so well last night." he replied with a devilishly handsome smile. "I may or may not have been comatose once my head hit the pillow."

Davis poured himself some coffee and leaned over the peninsula, resting his elbows on the countertop, his eyes trained on her with an impish grin on his face.

She took a bite of toast, chewed, and swallowed, feeling slightly self-conscious as he watched her so intently. "Are you not eating?" she asked, her eyebrow raised in question.

"I already have," he replied. "I like watching you eat, though."

Marnie flashed him an awkward grin and took a big bite of her toast, making him chuckle. Something about how his eyes fixed on her made her feel fluttery, like he was taking in all of her and appreciating what he saw. *But is he flirting or just being nice to her because he feels he has to be?* Honestly, she was sure it was the latter. She wasn't exactly what most men went for, especially a man like Davis, who was unquestionably way out of her league.

EVERY WEDNESDAY WAS "CINNAMON BUN DAY" at Everything you Knead. Without question, the most popular day of the week, Marnie always ensured she had lots of stock pre-baked to fill the showcases so she could concentrate all her time on the infamous confection the town of Primrose was head over heels in love with.

Putting another batch in the oven, she glanced at the clock to check the time. Marnie smiled, knowing her good friends, Bea Baxter, Whitney Hastings, and Ever Hastings were likely at their usual table visiting and enjoying the feature of the day. She washed her hands, grabbed a coffee pot, and went to the front to greet the gaggle of her favorite customers.

"Hey, Marnie, how are things going at the house with Davis?" Bea asked, giving her an amused grin as she came around the counter towards them.

Marnie's face instantly reddened with her question, and she wished she had better control of it. Stopping in front of their table, she put her hand on her hip, staring down at her friend. "You didn't warn me, Bea!"

"About what?" she asked with a chuckle as she feigned innocence.

"That your brother is a stone-cold fox!" Marnie exclaimed, fanning herself with her free hand.

Bea laughed and Marnie shook her head at her friend. Bea always loved to tease her and now she had direct ammunition.

"I haven't seen Davis since he was a 16-year-old kid." Ever said. "I assume from this conversation he has grown up?"

Bea pulled her phone out and scrolled through her pictures, then turned it around to show Ever and Whitney. Marnie glanced over, looking as well. *Damn, he's handsome.*

"Holy smokes, I would say so," Ever commented, as she leaned back in her seat, a look of surprise on her face.

"I may be married to the once hottest bachelor in Primrose, but even I have to admit he is one good-looking guy." Whitney added with a wiggle of her eyebrows.

"So, you see what I'm dealing with then!" Marnie exclaimed as she poured more coffee into Bea and Ever's mugs.

"Marnie, will you be my sister-in-law?" Bea teased, looking at Marnie with hopeful eyes and a little naughtiness behind her smile.

Marnie squinted at her friend, giving her a death glare, then with a smile, trying not to giggle, replied, "You are just plain mean." All the ladies laughed as she turned to greet a customer waiting at the counter.

Although Marnie knew Bea was just teasing, the thought of Davis and her made her temperature rise. Not only was he so handsome it made her eyes hurt, but he was so sweet. The way he made her breakfast this morning and took some time to visit with her before she left for work. The consideration he was giving her was heady, and she liked being the focus of his attention. It's just that she didn't know if it was genuine and part of her needed to be guarded not only for her self-esteem, but for her heart.

CHAPTER 3

"Hey Marnie!" Bea greeted as she walked into the bakery. It was their weekly meet up and Bea, fresh off her honeymoon in Ireland, radiated blissful happiness as she took a seat at the table with Whitney and Ever. Marnie leaned into Rami, letting him know she was going to take a break. She'd been at the bakery for five hours already and she was beyond exhausted. The long hours combined with the sleepless nights worrying about this pregnancy were wearing her down. The added stress of keeping this secret from her family and friends added to her exhaustion.

"Are you able to take a break and join us?" Ever asked as Marnie nodded and sank into the chair, letting out a long-drawn-out sigh.

"Cinnamon Bun Day, no need to say more, my friend," Bea commented, offering her a wary look. "But you look a little pale Marnie. Are you feeling okay?"

Marnie feigned a smile, appreciating her worry for her, but not wanting to expose her secret just yet. Bea was such a good friend and although they had only known each other for two years, she felt like she had known her so much longer. "I've been feeling a little under the weather lately." She replied. *Morning sickness will do that.* "Likely just from lack of sleep. This place has been hopping and I have custom orders coming out of my ears back there," she said, gesturing to her back kitchen. *Partially true.* "I may need to hire a baking assistant soon."

"Do it." Whitney urged. "Ever since Hayden got more help at the Hardware store, he has been so much happier and healthier."

"Yeah, I think I need to. Rami can't be here all the time now that Prairie Sound has been booking more gigs and they will probably be picked up by a tour soon. He also has been talking about moving in with his bandmate, Layne, so it'll be just me in the house."

"Do you need to rent out the extra room?" Bea asked. "I can put out some feelers for you."

"No, business is good, and I can afford the entire rent myself. It's just nice to have someone living there with me," Marnie replied.

"If you keep the room open, then Davis has a place to stay when he's on leave or back from his mission, whenever that may be." Ever added.

Bea crossed her arms over her chest and cocked her head at Marnie. "Speaking of Davis, he sent me an email asking me for your email address. Says he wants to get in contact with you. I was surprised at first since you two have spent so much time together and I figured he would already have your information."

More time than you realize, Bea. Marnie laughed, trying

to feign off her assumption. "Yes, you can give him my contact info, and Davis and I are just friends." All three of the ladies giggled and looked at each other knowingly. "What?" Marnie asked, not in on the joke.

"Marnie, you don't look at your friends like you want to do dirty things to them." Ever added with a smile, her eyebrows raised. "You have to admit, you two have a very intense energy when you're around each other, and we all know a little about that." Her three friends nodded in agreement.

Marnie wasn't sure why she kept denying her feelings towards Davis. *Why am I so naïve to think that others wouldn't notice?* They did have something very palpable and raw. A chemistry that was reactionary. Like a match ready to ignite. It was that chemistry that got them into her current predicament. Even though she didn't question whether Davis was attracted to her and had no doubt he cared for her, she was almost certain it was purely physical for him. Their night together was just him acting on his pent-up desire. For Marnie, that wonderful night meant more, as she was already very much aware that she was falling in love with him and the thought of him not reciprocating her feelings was something she needed to prepare for. Not just for herself, but for their baby.

* * *

DAVIS LOGGED into his email and waited impatiently for it to boot up. It had been a long hot day under the African sun, and he was exhausted. As a UN Peacekeeper with a Mechanical Engineering degree, he would work long hours on the construction site, helping to rebuild much needed infrastructure destroyed during war. Although his job was challenging, he loved it and knew his skill set was needed. Now showered and wearing clean fatigues, he scanned his email, finding several information emails about his mission and his weekly check in from Bea. His sister was back from her whirlwind honeymoon on the Emerald Isle and had sent him pictures. He scanned each picture, smiling as she posed in front of historic buildings and popular tourist spots. He stopped on one of her and her new husband, Garrett. The joy on her face made his heart swell with happiness for her. He loved and adored his sister and felt guilty about leaving her behind when he joined the military. Coming from tumultuous beginnings, they had always been close and acted as each other's protection and support. Two against the world. Looking at her photo now, seeing she was loved, taken care of, and living her best life with her new family was more than he could have hoped for her.

His mind drifted off to their wedding only five weeks ago when he walked her down the aisle to the love of her life. Correct that, halfway down the aisle, as Bea in pure Bea fashion made the rest of the walk or run on her own. He chuckled at the memory.

It had been nice to be back in Primrose, his home, no matter where the military sent him. Even if it was only for a week, it was nice to see everyone. Especially the woman he was most eager to see, Marnie Perez. The feisty, crazy sexy Latina living in his house. A woman he could stare at all day, taking in her endless curves and not feel one bit guilty about it. A woman with soft melting chocolate eyes that could disable him and a smart mouth that could silence him. *Damn that mouth.* Sweet, full lips that he yearned to kiss. He was like a moth to a flame around her, their attraction intense. His mind drifted to the night they spent together, finally acting on their fiery connection. A night they had waited for and could no longer deny themselves. Memories of that incredible night clouded his thoughts, literally giving him material for all his sexy dreams. Many a night he lay awake, unable to sleep, remembering how she felt under his hands, soft, subtle, perfection. She was everything he wanted, everything he desired, and just the kind of woman he would want to spend the rest of his life with.

Waking from his daydream, he heard the familiar notification ring on the computer. Closing Bea's email, he smiled, thanking the universe for reading his thoughts. An email from Marnie. Bea must have spoken to her.

Email from Marnie Perez @ Everything you Knead to Sergeant Davis Baxter, Canadian Armed Forces – UN Peacekeepers:

Hi Davis! I hope this email finds you well and safe. Bea said you wanted my email information and honestly, I'm not sure why I hadn't given it to you already. So here goes, email me anytime and if you need to call, here is my phone number. It would be wonderful to talk. I miss your voice. I'm sorry it's taken me so long to reach out to you. I think about you a lot these days and pray that you will be home again soon. Mostly I think about the night of Bea's wedding and wonder if you think about it too. That night was special to me, probably meaning more to me than it did to you. I really wish you were here so I could talk to you in person about it, but since this is as good as it will get for us, I need to tell you something. I'm pregnant.

Davis sat back in his seat and ran his hand over his face, then reread the last sentence in her email. *Marnie is pregnant. But we used protection. No wait a minute, did we?* Flashbacks of their night coming back to him in a rush. Realization dawning, he knew the answer to his question. No condom equals possible pregnancy. Now she was indeed pregnant. He needed to talk to her, but video calling was tricky out here. He needed to know what she was going to do. Was she going to have it? From what he knew of her family, having spent some time with them, he was sure she would. The Perez family were devoutly religious, so ending the pregnancy wasn't an option. He wouldn't want that anyway. She was having his baby; the thought making a rush of warmth he had never experienced fill his chest. Glancing down at the email, he noticed a picture attached. Clicking on it, a photo of a pregnancy test with two very clear, very pink lines popped up. He ran his hand through his hair and stared at the picture in disbelief. Ready or not, he was going to be a daddy.

MARNIE WAITED two days to hear from Davis, two whole excruciatingly long days and nights. Not able to sleep, she lay awake wondering what he thought of her email, what he thought of her news. She buried her face in her pillow and screamed into it. *Why did I just send it out like that? Oh,*

by the way, I'm pregnant. You're going to be a dad. Estupido. Knowing sleep was elusive, she rolled out of bed and padded down the hall to the kitchen. Flicking on the light, she squinted as she glanced at the kitchen clock: 11 p.m. *Not too late for cake.* Cutting herself a slice of her latest experiment, Pumpkin Praline Cheesecake, and pouring herself a large glass of milk, she settled herself into a kitchen chair and stared at her closed laptop. She sat there and savored her cake, trying to will herself not to check for the millionth time for his response. *Just one more time.* Her willpower breaking, she flipped her laptop open. Impatiently, she let the dated laptop boot up and she opened her email account. Her heart leapt as she saw his name on the screen. Sergeant Davis Baxter, Canadian Armed Forces – UN Peacekeeper. Her finger hovered over the key, and a sense of dread enveloped her. *What if he's unhappy or, God forbid, thinks the baby isn't his? What if he wants me to end the pregnancy? No way am I going to do that. I am having this baby!* Taking a deep breath and letting it out slowly, she pressed the button, closing her eyes, not wanting to look. With every possible worst-case scenario and response running through her head, she slowly opened her eyes to read his email.

Marry Me.

Marnie nearly fell off her chair. Never in a million years did she expect that response. *He must be losing his mind. Is he crazy? Is he joking? If he is, it's not funny.* As much as she was scared to tell her family about her pregnancy out of wedlock, she wasn't going to marry someone that didn't love her back. Baby Daddy or not. Her unrequited love or not. She immediately clicked the reply button.

Email from Marnie Perez @ Everything you Knead to Davis Baxter, Canadian Armed Forces – UN Peace-keepers:

Hi Davis! Have you lost your ever-loving mind? Marry you? I mean, I appreciate you wanting to do the right thing, but I'm not marrying someone that doesn't love me. I know you like me, but I don't think you love me.

She read over her words again. He had to know how crazy he sounded. They hadn't even officially dated, and she had so much more to learn about him. He wasn't the most forthcoming and was very guarded. He liked to ask the questions, not answer them, even though she had a way of making him open up. Ding, a notification.

Marnie, I've never been more serious in my life. I want to marry you. Not only as it's the right thing to do, but it's some-thing I WANT to do. If you say yes, I don't know when I'll be home next. I can apply for leave again in 6 months. Will you wait till then? I promise you, this is not just me being an honor-able guy. I care about you Marnie, very deeply and now I care about our baby.

Marnie stared at the screen for a long time, not sure how to reply. On the one hand, he confirmed he wasn't experiencing a moment of insanity and on the other hand; it wasn't exactly a declaration of love either. But he said it, he cared deeply for her and their unborn child. *Is that good enough for me? Could I settle for that and hope he would one day fall in love with me? Is it a chance I'm willing to take?*

Marnie knew her answer, she needed to do the right thing for their baby and selfishly for her own heart. Mind racing and heart pounding against her chest, she typed her answer.

Yes, Davis, I will marry you.

CHAPTER 4

A year and a half ago – Christmas Eve

Marnie woke, feeling rested and accomplished. Her first holiday season at Everything You Knead was now done and a resounding success. She was so proud of her business and was so grateful for Primrose and the surrounding area for supporting her. Now, she had three days off before opening again on the 27th and she was going to enjoy it thoroughly. Navidad was her favorite time of year, and her family went all out. The usual barrage of gifts and far too much food and drink were likely on the agenda. She couldn't wait, but for now she needed to get up because she, of course, was making the desserts for the festivities. Climbing out of bed, she glanced at her clock. 6:35 a.m., internally congratulating herself on sleeping in. Slipping out of her bedroom, she made her way down the hallway to the bathroom to take care of morning needs. Brushing her teeth, washing her face, and pulling her wavy hair into a messy bun, she quickly took in her reflection before she exited the bathroom. Flicking off the light, she turned and ran right into Davis. Letting out a surprised squeak, she looked down at her hands splayed on his rock-hard chest and her eyes slowly drifted up to meet his playful gaze.

"Are you done in the bathroom?" he asked, his voice deep and husky.

Marnie wasn't sure if she could speak, suddenly very aware of her own heartbeat thrumming against her chest. This was the first time she had seen him shirtless, and the view did not disappoint. He was huge, his muscles tight and sinewy, with veins popping from his bulky biceps. She had never had a particular type of man she was attracted to, but looking at Davis, she knew she was attracted. Immediately, Marnie's gaze zoned in on the ink tattooed on his left pectoral. A shamrock with the words family, courage, loyalty, and strength written within. The tattoo looked 3D as if it was trying to tear through his skin. Boldly Marnie grazed her fingertips over his tattoo, wondering if she could feel the rise of the skin and the texture of a scar. "I love this," she said softly, her fingertips tracing the words. He met her gaze, his green eyes darkening as he settled his hand on her waist. The heat of his hand shot straight to her core, making her body instantly flush with warmth. She swallowed and met his gaze, now flaming with restrained desire. "I just have never seen anything like it," she whispered.

"Do you have any ink?" he asked, his voice rough.

"I do." She replied, turning to show him, her sleep tank dipping low in the back exposing her tattoo. Between her shoulder blades, three brightly colored gardenias were inked, along with words that were meaningful to her.

"Mia familia," he said as he ran his rough fingertips over the words, making goosebumps rise on her skin and causing her to shiver. "My family?"

She smiled and nodded as he touched the flowers, gently tracing their lines. "One is for my Abuela, one is for Mia Madre, and I am the one in the middle. I have all brothers and we're the only women in the family. I put it on my back as they always have my back."

"I like that. It's beautiful."

Marnie turned, meeting his intense gaze, feeling an invisible pull between them, and wanting nothing more in the world than for him to kiss her right now. He glanced down at her lips, then back to her eyes and she could tell he felt that pull too. Maybe it was their close proximity the past four days, maybe it was the sweet gestures, the early morning talks over coffee, the way he looked at her and made her feel truly seen, but here in this moment all she needed was the touch of his lips on hers. She put her hand over his tattoo, splaying it over his chest, and she could feel his heart beating wildly under her palm. He reached up with his free hand and moved a strand of hair from her face, then slid his large palm behind her head, making her breath hitch and skin sizzle. Davis, taking notice of her reaction, smiled, drawing his mouth impossibly closer. She instinctively darted her tongue out and wet her bottom lip, his eyes following the sweep of her tongue as he asked. "Can I kiss you, Marnie?" His husky voice dripped with need.

"Yes." she replied breathlessly.

He leaned in slowly, bridging the gap between them, their breaths mingling hot and heady, as he brushed his lips over hers. The kiss was featherlike and so excruciatingly gentle. Her body grew hot, begging for more, but he kissed her respectfully, keeping boundaries yet making sure she knew how much he desired her. His hand on her waist ran up her back, touching the skin above her sleeping tank, and she was now painfully aware of her lack of bra, her barely covered breasts peaked and heavy, pressing against his hard chest. The contrast of his hardness against her softness made her ridiculously aroused.

THE MOMENT DAVIS touched his lips to Marnie's, he felt a jolt of electricity through him. She tasted like sugar, so sweet, so soft, so sensual, her supple lips like heaven as they kissed. He'd fantasized about this moment so many times over the past four days and right now here in this hallway, he wanted nothing more than to back her into the wall and press the length of his body against her, or perhaps back her into his room so he could lay her out and worship her gorgeous body. *She is everything.* Their mouths moved together in a slow sensual rhythm, a kiss he would dream about in the future on those lonely days while on a mission. But he needed to be a gentleman, not push his desire for her too far. He needed to hold himself back and be respectful of her boundaries. He had the feeling she wasn't the kind of girl to fall into bed with a guy, especially a guy she was just getting to know, and he would not make her feel uncomfortable.

Releasing their kiss, she gazed up at him, her face flushed, lips plumb and rosy and her melting chocolate eyes in a post kiss haze. "That was…" she started.

"Amazing." Davis added, tucking a stray strand of hair behind her ear and cupping her cheek. "You are so beautiful, Sugar."

Marnie's eyes flashed with amusement at the term of endearment. "Sugar?" she questioned, an eyebrow raised.

"Because your lips taste like sugar," he replied, running the pad of his thumb over her bottom lip.

She smiled, licked where he touched, and let out a sigh. "Speaking of sugar, I have desserts to make for Navidad tonight."

Arms securing around her waist, he beamed down on her as he asked, "Would you like my help?"

"Do you want to?" she questioned; an eyebrow raised.

"Of course," he replied with a grin. "Spend time with you, learn all your secrets and get to taste test? Yes, please."

Marnie glanced down at his low-slung sleep pants and replied, "Go get dressed and meet me in the kitchen in 10 minutes." She said as she wriggled out of his hold and stepped around him to her bedroom door. Glancing over her shoulder, she added. "And be ready to work, because you are now my assistant."

MARNIE COULDN'T REMEMBER a time she had such an enjoyable day. Baking together had proven to be an amazing way to get to know Davis better. He was funny, flirtatious, and genuinely wanted to learn from her. He asked countless questions and followed her lead, making them a great team in the kitchen. Plus, the sight of him wearing a frilly pink apron with his bulky frame and muscles popping was a sight she would not soon forget.

Finishing, baking supplies put away and dishes drying in the dish rack, they sat together at the kitchen table nursing their cups of coffee. Marnie glanced at Davis, grateful for his help. Having been raised to always thank those that went out of their way for you and not wanting to end this building connection between them too soon, an idea came to mind on how she could thank him. "What are you doing tonight? Does Bea have plans for you?"

"Church and a gathering at Prairie Sky Acres, I think. Why are you asking?" he replied, a curious smile curving his lips, as he raised his cup of coffee and took a sip.

Suddenly feeling nervous about what she was about to ask, she stuttered, "Well, I…I mean, I was wondering if you would like to come celebrate Navidad with my family. I mean, I wouldn't want to take you away from any other plans you have, but I really appreciated your help today, and I think you might enjoy yourself."

"It sounds like fun."

"It is!" she exclaimed excitedly. "There's so much food, drinks flowing, gifts, music, maybe some dancing." His smile grew wider as she added. "I do have to warn you though, my family is very loud and a little loco."

Davis laughed, his deep rich voice doing strange and wonderful things to her body. "Well then, now I have to go. They sound like people I need to get to know."

Marnie grinned at his response, an excitement

building within her at the thought of spending the evening with Davis and bringing him to meet her family even if they were just friends. *Friends generally don't kiss each other like that.* Mind reeling with questions, she stared into her coffee cup now, wondering if that kiss meant something different to her than it did to him.

* * *

"HOLA, FAMILIA!" Marnie exclaimed as they entered Abuela's house. "Feliz Navidad!"

Loud laughter and music filled the home along with the delicious smells of slow cooked meats, rich spicy sauces and chilis. Marnie smiled at Davis; his arms laden with bakery boxes filled with the desserts they made. "Come with me, it's so loud in here, I don't think they heard us arrive. Hola, Feliz Navidad!" Marnie exclaimed again, entering what looked like a large living room.

Everyone's heads turned as they acknowledged Marnie first, all eyes drifting over to Davis standing beside her. And there were a lot of eyes. Her family was large, making even Davis, a sergeant in the military, a little intimidated.

"Everyone, this is Sergeant Davis Baxter, a friend of mine and our guest here tonight." Marnie introduced commanding the room. "This is his first Navidad, so let's all make him feel welcome."

The room was quiet a moment before a chorus of greetings came from the crowd, as several young men approached him, taking the boxes from his hands one by one, Marnie scolding them in Spanish as they disappeared with the desserts. *Her brothers?* A short, stout woman with beautiful long grey hair, twisted back and pinned by an ornate clip, rich brown eyes like Marnie and deep smile lines entered the room with her arms outstretched in greeting. "

"Davis, Hola! I'm Marnie's Abuela. Welcome to my home! Feliz Navidad!" she greeted, with a bright smile, taking his hands in hers and stretching up on her toes to plant a kiss on his cheek. She beamed at him with such kindness and warmth that instantly Davis knew he liked this woman.

Abuela let go of his hands and turned her attention to Marnie, embracing her as she did him. "Such a handsome young man you've brought with you, Mila." she said, giving her a wink before she took both of their hands and led them into the kitchen, the table covered with more heavenly food than Davis had ever seen.

* * *

DAVIS GLANCED over at Marnie in the passenger's seat. She was a little drunk and a whole lot cute. When she invited him to join in on her family's Navidad celebration, he had no idea what to expect. Her exceedingly generous family welcomed him in and within minutes he had a plate of food, a cerveza in hand and felt like he was part of the family. They had a true sense of love and community that he had never experienced before, and he had enjoyed himself thoroughly.

Turning into the driveway, Davis parked and glanced at the beautiful woman in the passenger seat. She had her head turned toward him, her eyes glassy from too much holiday merriment and he surveyed her considering how he was going to get her into the house. Davis was never a huge drinker, so when the tequila was passed around and he noticed she wasn't holding back tonight, he made the choice to stop so she could let loose and have some fun.

Marnie gave him a coquettish smile. "Did I tell you how hot I think you are?"

Davis laughed, a deep rumble from his chest and he offered her an amused smile, as this was the third time she'd told him this since he managed to get her into the vehicle. "Yes, Sugar, you did."

"Well, you are. You are sooo crazy hot; I just want to kiss you again and this time maybe grab your tight ass," she said, putting her hand to her mouth. "Oops, did I say that?" she asked, covering her mouth with her hand, muffling a little giggle followed by a hiccup.

Dear Lord, she's adorable. He just shook his head with a chuckle and exited the car, coming around the passenger's side to help her out. Opening her door, she ungracefully exited the car, and he put an arm around her, trying to keep her upright. "I had too much tequila tonight." she whispered into his ear; her breath deliciously warm against his skin.

"I know, Sugar." he replied, helping her down the walkway and with some effort up the porch steps successfully.

She leaned against him, her body so close it made his pulse spike at the proximity as he unlocked the door.

Stumbling inside, she exclaimed, "I had so much fun tonight!"

"I did too. Thank you for inviting me," he said, meeting her gaze as he flipped the lock of the door and helped her out of her winter coat, crouching down to unzip her boots.

She watched him, leaning against the front entrance wall as he helped her out of her boots and rose to his feet. Eyes locked on his, Marnie looped her arms around his neck and let out a sigh as she said. "Everyone loved you." He smiled as she ran her hand over his jaw, dipping into the cleft, her eyes flitting to his, her face turning serious. "I think I love you."

Davis internally shook his head and laughed at her drunken declaration. *She is so going to regret this in the morning.* "Sugar, as much as I like our sweet words, I think you need to sleep off the tequila."

She frowned and jutted her lip out in a pout as he helped her down the hallway to her room. Opening her door, he helped her inside and brought her to the bed, encouraging her to sit down. She complied, and he turned to go towards the door.

"I'm just going to get you some Tylenol, some water and a garbage can in case you get sick, okay," he informed, lingering at the door.

She nodded in response, and he ducked out of the room. Retrieving the Tylenol, the bathroom garbage can, and pouring her a glass of water, he returned to her bedroom. As he entered, he stopped dead in his tracks. Somehow, in the short time he was gone, she managed to strip off all her clothes and was now sprawled on top of the comforter, in just her bra and panties. He internally groaned at the sight of her luscious body on display, and he couldn't help but take in the swell of her beautiful breasts, the dip of her waist and her gorgeous round behind. Marnie was sex personified and she too, was asleep, her breaths coming out slowly and steadily. He laughed quietly to himself at the position he was now in. Putting the water and Tylenol on the nightstand, he shimmied the covers back on the bed as much as he could. Then coming around her side, he slid his arms under her body and lifted her. Her body instantly melted into his, and she let out a deep sigh as he held her against his chest. Lingering a moment with her in his arms, he looked down, taking in her beautiful face, so peaceful and content. He laid her under the covers, taking one last self-satisfying look at her curvaceous body and pulled the comforter over her. *That body will give me something to dream about tonight.* Quietly Davis headed towards the door and as he was about to exit, Marnie let out a long-drawn-out moan and he turned, his eyebrows raised.

"Oh Davis," she moaned. He glanced at her, his ears perking and his lips curving into an amused smile. *Yes, she's definitely going to regret this in the morning.*

MARNIE WOKE THE NEXT DAY, her head pounding like a jackhammer. She squinted at the alarm clock, shocked to see the time said 8:43 a.m. She shivered and pulled her comforter tight over her shoulders. Suddenly, the realization of why she was so cold hit her and she raised the comforter to find herself in nothing but her bra and panties. She did a double take and groaned, clutching her head. *How did I get undressed? Who brought me to bed?* Marnie buried her face in her pillow and groaned. *Davis.*

Just then, a knock sounded at her door. She sat up, covering her body with the comforter, wishing she hadn't gotten up so quickly, her head spinning like a top. "Come in." She replied, feigning brightness, although she felt anything but bright at the moment.

Davis strode in carrying a tray with what smelled like coffee and hot buttered toast, a huge smile plastered on his handsome face. "Merry Christmas." he said, setting the tray on the bed in front of her.

"Feliz Navidad" she answered, clutching the comforter to her chest, and meeting his gaze with a look of gratitude on her face. "Thank you for this," she said, gesturing to the tray.

"You're welcome," he replied with a sweet smile as he turned on his heel to leave.

"Davis, wait." He turned instantly, his eyes pinning hers. "Can you please grab me a t-shirt from the top drawer?" she asked, hesitantly.

Davis strode over to her dresser, opened the drawer, pulled out a long blue T-shirt, showing her and with her approval, he brought it over to her.

She glanced up at him, a sheepish look on her face. "I know you've probably seen the goods already, but can you turn around so I can put this on?" she asked, gesturing for him to turn around. He obliged, the twinkle in his eyes giving away his amusement. "Okay, I'm decent." She said, and he turned back to face her. "Have a seat."

He sat down on the bed gently so as not to spill her coffee and watched her take a bite of her toast.

She gave him a timid grin, then asked, "How drunk was I last night?"

"Pretty drunk," he replied with a low, rumbly laugh. "But you're pretty cute and very chatty when you're drunk, so I didn't mind."

Marnie's cheeks heated with embarrassment as she covered her face and peeked through her fingers at him. "What did I say?"

He held up his hand and started ticking off his fingers. "Oh, Davis, you're so hot. Davis, do you know how hot you are? I think you're so hot, Davis. Kiss me. Just to name a few."

Marnie's eyes widened, and she whispered, "I am mortified."

"Don't be," he said with a laugh, then cocked his eyebrow at her. "At least I know what you think of me."

"You didn't know already from our kiss yesterday?" she asked, feeling a little audacious.

"That helped, yes, but also the "I think I love you" and the "Oh Davis!" you moaned in your sleep as I was leaving your room gave me a little better indication as to how you feel."

"Que chingados!" she exclaimed, grabbing a pillow and putting it over her face.

Davis let out a deep laugh and reached for the pillow, taking it away from her, then setting it back down beside her. "It's okay Marnie. I know you were drunk, so I'm not taking your comments seriously."

Marnie just shook her head, her face a burning inferno as she asked, "Did you at least have fun last night?"

"I had an amazing time," he replied. "Thank you for

inviting me. I have never experienced such hospitality before. Your family is incredible."

Marnie took in his words and smiled, knowing how welcoming and gracious her family was. Turning her expression serious, she asked with a twinkle and a tug of a smile on her lips, "Now please tell me how I ended up half naked?"

CHAPTER 5

"Knock knock!" Bea exclaimed, entering her grandmother's house. "Marnie, are you here?"

"Yes, sorry, just give me a few minutes. I'll be right out," Marnie shouted from down the hallway. Flushing away the evidence of her sickness, she grabbed her toothbrush and scrubbed away the putrid taste. This was the 8th time she had brushed her teeth today, and she was tired of it. Morning sickness was no joke, but who was she kidding? It was all day sickness in her case. Turning on the faucet, she splashed cold water on her face and reached for a towel dabbing at her face. Catching her eyes in the mirror, she took in her reflection. She was pale and her eyes looked tired, with dark shadows underneath. *You can't keep this secret forever.* Mustering the courage to exit the bathroom, she came around the corner into the kitchen to see Bea waiting for her on a stool by the peninsula scrolling through her phone.

Bea set her phone down, took one look at her appearance and frowned. "Still not feeling well?" Bea asked, her eyebrows furrowed in concern.

Marnie nodded and gave her an imploring look. Bea folded her arms over her chest and squinted at her friend, surveying her for a moment, then said, "Spill."

Marnie took a deep breath and swallowed as she confessed, "I'm pregnant, and Davis is the father."

Bea unfolded her arms and put her palms down on the counter, her head bowed a moment, then looked up at Marnie. "Say what?"

"Davis and I slept together the night of your wedding and now I'm pregnant."

Bea's eyes widened, and she sat there a moment quietly just staring at Marnie, slowly blinking and when she spoke her voice was low, almost a whisper. "Does Davis know?"

"Yes, I told him as soon as you gave me his contact information." Marnie answered. "And then he asked me to marry him." She added, wincing and waiting for the onslaught she knew was coming from her now future sister-in-law.

"Holy crap!" Bea exclaimed, hopping off the stool and pacing back and forth. "What did you say?"

"I said yes." Marnie replied. "I thought about it, and it seemed like the right thing to do, considering the situation."

"But do you love him? Does he love you?" she asked pointedly, needing to know more.

"He says he cares deeply for me, and I'm falling in love

with him, Bea. I've felt this way for a while, but I've never been in love before, and… oh Bea, I am so confused." Marnie said, putting her hands over her face, feeling a rush of emotion rise in her chest as hot tears pricked her eyes. Warm, reassuring hands settled on her shoulders, and she lowered her hands from her face, letting them fall to her sides with defeat. Slowly, she opened her eyes to be met by Bea's compassionate gaze.

"It's going to be okay, Marnie." Bea said, offering her a reassuring smile. "I'll help you in any way I can. And know that my brother is an honest man and never says anything he doesn't mean. If he says he wants to marry you and cares deeply for you, he does. He wants to take care of you and the baby."

Emotion bubbled over, Marnie's chin started trembling as Bea wrapped her arms around her and she buried her face, all her uncertain tears spilling out onto her friend's shoulder.

* * *

Email from Marnie Perez @ Everything you Knead to Sergeant Davis Baxter, Canadian Armed Forces – UN Peacekeepers:

Davis,

I hope you're well, and this email finds you safe. I confirmed the pregnancy last week. 8 weeks along today. I've been giving a lot of thought to your proposal, and I want you to know I didn't expect it. I can't help but think you only asked out of responsibility and obligation. Call me naïve, but I felt something between us, and it wasn't just lust for me. I think of you all the time and pray every day that you're safe and will come home soon. I'm trying not to get too excited about marrying you as I still have so many mixed feelings about it. I have so many mixed feelings about everything these days. I know a baby is a blessing, so maybe it's hormones or the fact that I'm going into this alone, but I can't stop crying. Perhaps it's the little sleep I get these days. I dream of you all night long and just wish you were here, wrapping your strong arms around me, comforting me, and telling me it's all going to be okay. I haven't said anything to my family and luckily, they have no clue yet. That's going to be a hard conversation. I want you to know I told Bea. I needed someone here to talk about all of this. As much as I love your emails, I needed someone to physically talk to. Someone I can trust. Your sister is amazing, and I wanted to give you a heads up as you will likely have an email from her soon. Sorry. Love Marnie

Email from Sergeant Davis Baxter, Canadian Armed Forces – UN Peacekeepers to Marnie Perez @ Everything you Knead:

Marnie,

I have been thinking about you a lot too and our baby. I know my proposal seems impulsive, but I am truly honored you said yes. I want to take care of you and our child, and I wish I could be there to wipe your tears away and hold you. I too dream of you. Both of you in fact. I wonder what he/she will look like. Will our child have red hair? Will our child have your beautiful brown eyes? Remembering your eyes and your beautiful smile helps get me through the hard days here. So, if you doubt I feel

more for you than lust, just know I do. I feel a lot for you,
Marnie. So much more than you probably realize.
PS Thank you for the heads up on Bea. I'm sure a strongly
worded email is coming my way soon.
Always on my mind,
Davis

Email from Beatrix Baxter-Smithfield to Sergeant Davis
Baxter, Canadian Armed Forces – UN Peacekeeper:
Hey Bro!
Well, well, well, I feel like I should yell at you, perhaps scream,
stomp, and shout. Say something like "Damn you brother for
knocking up my friend!" Yes, I'm not going to lie, I considered
doing that, but I know you're a grown ass man and after talking
to Marnie, you're taking your responsibility to her seriously. So
instead of ripping you up, I want to congratulate you. I'm truly
happy for you. Although this whole thing is kind of backwards,
know that I'm proud of how you're stepping up. Marnie has
such a good and pure heart, so please don't break it. I know you
can be a broody beast sometimes and that isn't what she needs
from you going forward. She needs someone who is forthcoming
and will love and cherish her. She deserves the best, so make
sure you give her the best of you.
Your mildly ticked off sister,
Bea

Email from Sergeant Davis Baxter, Canadian Armed
Forces – UN Peacekeeper to Beatrix Baxter-Smithfield
Bea,
Are you getting all mushy on me now, Sis? Whatever happened
to my blunt and opinionated sister? I appreciate you not yelling

at me for this. Honestly, I'm still processing everything but despite that I promise you, I know what I'm doing. I know how special Marnie is, and all I want is to make her happy. Speaking of that, I need a favor from you. I want to know if you know where Nanner's ring is. She left it for me to give to my wife to be and I was hoping you could track it down. I left it in the house and know you went through everything before you moved out. I'm also trying to arrange a video call with Marnie to ask her to marry me, officially. I wondered if you could be there when I do so you could give her the ring? Your help and support mean everything to me, Bea. I still cannot believe I'm going to be a dad and someday soon a husband.
Davis

Email from Beatrix Baxter-Smithfield to Col. Davis Baxter, Armed Forces Canada – UN Peacekeeper:
Davis,
I have the ring! I found it when I was cleaning out the house and put it aside for you. Nanners would be proud of you. When did you get so sentimental and sweet? I think Marnie would really like you to officially ask her and I'm happy to help in whatever way you need me to. Tell me when and where and I'll be there. And Davis, try to make this romantic. Marnie deserves the world.
Bea

"Have a great day, ladies!" Rami winked flirtatiously at a group of female customers.

Marnie shook her head and let out a laugh. Her handsome and charming brother sure was good for business and she wasn't complaining. She was having a good day today. The morning sickness was being kind to her, and she was finally feeling a little more like her old self again. At 12 weeks pregnant, she hoped that it was starting to subside. Keeping her pregnancy from Rami and the rest of the family had proven to be difficult, but so far, so good, no one seemed to suspect anything. Although Marnie didn't doubt they loved her and would support her no matter what; she wasn't quite ready for their nosy questions and meddling ways.

"Hey, Marnie!" Bea exclaimed, coming through the swinging doors of the kitchen, a laptop under her arm.

"Do you think you could take a 30-minute break? I was thinking you and I could talk in your office. I have something to show you," she told her, a huge smile on her face.

"Yeah, I think I could take a bit of a break," Marnie replied curiously. "Just let me wash up and I'll meet you there in about 5 minutes."

Bea nodded and disappeared into her office.

Marnie let Rami know she was taking a break and went to wash up. When she returned and entered her office, she saw Bea sitting in her office chair, her laptop open on her desk and a conspiring twinkle in her eyes. She put her hand on her hip and giggled as she stared down at her friend and asked, "What are you up to, Bea?"

Bea smiled at her, turned to face the screen, and gave her laptop a wink, then got up from the chair, gesturing for Marnie to take a seat. Curiously, Marnie obliged and glanced at the screen of the open laptop. There on the screen was Davis's impossibly handsome face.

"Davis!" Marnie exclaimed in surprise, her hand

instinctively reaching out to touch his face on the screen. "You look so good."

"So do you, Sugar. How are you feeling?" he asked, his brows drawing together in concern.

"Today has been good, but it's been difficult. Morning sickness is more like all day sickness for me."

He frowned and replied. "I wish I could be there for you. How is our little one doing?"

"12 weeks today and I have my first prenatal appointment tomorrow." She said, offering him a wistful smile as she met his gorgeous green eyes on the screen. "We'll find out the due date and be able to hear the heartbeat."

"I wish I could be there to hear it," he said, giving her a half smile, regret in his tone. "Email me and let me know how it goes. I want to know everything."

"I will." she answered with a resigned smile.

"I don't have much time here on video, and it can be spotty, but I wanted to see your beautiful face." Marnie smiled as he continued. "I know my proposal wasn't the most romantic and you deserve something special, at least as special as I can make it from here," he said, offering her a sincere smile. "Marnie, you, and I still have a lot to learn about one another and we're kind of doing things backwards here, but I want to know everything about you. Yes, maybe this baby has sped things up a bit for us, but if I wasn't deployed, I would want to date you, Marnie. And spend all my nights with you…" he added, flashing her a coquettish grin as he continued, "… and eventually I'm confident this is where we would end up. I can't promise you that we won't have challenges, but I want to face each challenge with you by my side. The other thing I'm sure of is that we both have strong feelings for each other, and I want you to hold on to that when I can't be with you. So, with all of that being said, please know that I want this, and I want you. This is not the first time I've asked, but consider this the time that counts. Marnie, will you marry me?"

Bea stepped forward and put a velvet ring box on her desk in front of her and Marnie looked up at her friend. Bea gave her a wink, gestured for her to open it, and took a step back. Marnie reached for the box and held it in her hands for a moment, taking in the velvety feel of the antique ring box. With trembling hands, she slowly opened the box to find a beautiful antique gold ring with a green stone in the middle surrounded by diamonds. The stone, a gorgeous emerald green, the color of Davis's eyes. Tears brimmed, and emotion rose in her chest as she took the ring out of the box and held it up, the stones catching the light as they twinkled. Marnie smiled and met Davis's gaze on the screen, as she wiped away a rogue tear that escaped down her cheek.

"This was my grandmother's ring, and she gave it to me to give to my future wife. What do you say?" he asked, his eyes hopeful. "Will you marry me, Sugar?"

Marnie looked down again at the gorgeous ring and knew in her heart what her answer was. "My answer is still yes, Davis. This ring is beautiful, and I'm so honored to wear it."

Davis beamed across the screen as his connection glitched. "Sorry, I'm losing…connect… ema…me" he said as the screen froze and went blank. A no connection notification band appeared across the bottom.

Marnie looked up at Bea, who was standing beside her with tears in her eyes and a look of disappointment on her face at the loss of the connection. Marnie looked down at the beautiful ring she was still holding, slipped it on her ring finger, and smiled. I guess this made it official. She was engaged to be married to Sergeant Davis Baxter.

CHAPTER 6

A year and a half ago – 2 days after Christmas

arnie was back at work after three wonderful days filled with family, friends, and lots and lots of Davis. She was getting used to having him around and thoroughly enjoyed his company. Yes, he was awesome to look at, but she loved his personality, too. Not only did he have the most interesting stories, but he was so incredibly smart and funny. They would find themselves talking and laughing for hours, late into the evening, losing track of time. As for their kiss in the hallway, they had yet to repeat that moment, and in some ways Marnie was glad. Although she relived that kiss over and over in her head, the reality was that kissing him again was a bad idea. He was leaving in seven days, and she knew in her heart she couldn't get too attached. Maybe if he stayed, they would start dating as the attraction was undoubtedly there, but with his time here in Primrose ticking down she figured keeping him in the friend zone was probably for the best.

Today was a quieter day. Marnie had a few regulars come in for coffee and treats and a few pickups, but all in all, she could tell people were still celebrating the holidays or recovering from them. The bell on the bakery door chimed, and she grabbed a dish towel to wipe her hands as she entered the front of the bakery. Davis stood by the counter looking every bit the sexy hunk that he was, dressed in a black bomber style jacket, a blue Henley underneath and dark wash jeans that hugged his muscular thighs.

"Miss me already?" Marnie teased, liking the comfort they now had to banter and flirt.

"Definitely." he answered with a wink. "I'm not going to be around tonight because I have plans with Bea and Garrett, so I thought I would come keep you company this afternoon. If you want the company, of course. I can help too if you need to put me to work," he said, rubbing his hands together. "I'm a great assistant baker, as you already know."

"I don't have a lot to do today, but you can join me in the kitchen. I'm just decorating cupcakes for an order." She answered with a smile as she gestured for him to come behind the counter.

Davis followed her into the large commercial kitchen, and his eyes widened as his gaze darted around the room, taking in all her equipment, pans, and tools neatly stacked and organized on the shelves. "Wow, this kitchen is amazing."

"Thank you. I'm proud of it," she said, looking around

at all that was hers. "Not many 24-year-olds can say they accomplished this."

"So, you're 24?" he asked, as if she had just shared some top-secret information about herself.

"And you are?" she countered curiously.

"28," he replied. "So, not too much older."

Marnie laughed at that comment and gave him a playful grin. "So, I'm not too much younger?"

"Touche. I've been wondering something about you," he said as she picked up a decorator bag. "What is a beautiful, 24-year-old, successful business owner who makes the best damn chocolate cake I've ever tasted doing single?" he asked, retrieving a second stool and taking a seat across from her. "You must have men lining up to date you."

Marnie lifted her head from what she was doing and let out a loud guffaw, then rolled her eyes.

He mirrored her laughter, his face somewhat puzzled at her reaction, and asked, "Seriously, what's the deal?"

She looked at him and sighed a resigned sigh. "I'm not exactly everyone's type." She answered simply. "Don't get me wrong, I've dated, but the consensus has always been, "you are so nice" or "you are so sweet" which in my experience is code for "you don't look like a supermodel"."

Davis shook his head and met her gaze. "Estupido!" he exclaimed.

Marnie's eyes widened with amusement, and she let out a little giggle. "Did you just say idiots in Spanish?"

"I did," he replied proudly. "Seriously, they're all a bunch of idiots if they didn't pursue you. In my eyes, you're perfect in every way."

Marnie took in his nice words and gave him a look of thanks. "If only all men thought that way. I mean, I like the way I look; I would much rather have curves and eat cake, anyway."

"Let them eat cake," he declared, making her giggle again.

"So, what about you? Any girlfriends, ladies in various ports, wild and crazy trysts? Or is it hard to date while on a mission?" she asked with genuine interest.

"I've dated, mostly when I've been home, but honestly, nothing major. I was a late bloomer and joined the army at 18, so my dating life was and is pretty minimal."

"What's your type?" she asked, curiously.

"You." he replied, without hesitation. Marnie lifted her eyes to him, searching for sincerity, only to be met with honesty. She let out a nervous giggle, feigning off his comment, and continued piping icing onto a tray of cupcakes. "My type is a woman who is smart, strong, independent and values family and loyalty. Physically, I like a woman I can hold on to at night. Someone with curves and imperfections. That's what I find sexy." Marnie's face flushed hot at his description. She knew what he was doing, and she wasn't used to someone being so forward with her and pursuing her like this. "Oh, and a woman that can bake a mean chocolate cake," he added with a wink. "If I found all of that, I would be crazy not to snap her up and make her mine."

* * *

"I'M SO NERVOUS." Marnie said as she sat waiting for the OB/GYN to come into the room.

Bea had taken the seat next to her and placed a reassuring hand on her shoulder. This was her first official prenatal appointment since confirming her pregnancy and she appreciated Bea coming along as support.

"They're just going to ask you a bunch of health questions and since you are about 12 weeks along, they'll check the heartbeat."

"Sounds easy enough." Marnie replied as the doctor entered the room.

"Bea." the middle-aged female doctor said as she took a seat at her desk and pulled up Marnie's chart. "Nice to see you again. I assume you're here for moral support." She said, glancing between Bea and Marnie with a welcoming smile. "Hi Marnie, I'm Dr. Danville. I understand this is your first prenatal appointment. Congratulations!"

"Thank you. I'm kind of nervous." Marnie confessed, letting out a long exhale.

"Don't be. This first appointment is easy, and we should be able to get your baby's heartbeat on the Doppler if you're as far along as you say you are," she said, giving her a kind smile. "I promise painless stuff."

Marnie nodded as Dr. Danville went through some routine questions about her general health, her family history and when she was sure she conceived, and she confirmed her estimated due date as April 29th the following year.

"Okay, now I will have you lie down on the examining table so we can hear that heartbeat."

"I'm excited!" Marnie exclaimed as she made herself comfortable and Dr. Danville pulled up her shirt and rolled down the front of her leggings to expose her lower abdomen.

"At 12 weeks we should be able to find it quickly." the doctor said with a smile as she squirted a clear gel on her stomach and ran the Doppler over her abdomen, side to side, up and down, a faint sound of static filling the room. The doctor's brows furrowed, and she stole a glance at Bea whose eyes were transfixed on the doctors. She tried for a few minutes, giving Marnie a half smile, then pulled the Doppler off her abdomen before speaking. "It's strange to not get a heartbeat at this stage of your pregnancy, so I would like you to have an internal ultrasound done today if possible," she said as she wiped the gel from her abdomen.

Marnie's eyes darted to Bea, whose face had taken on a sullen pallor. Bea looked away, not meeting her eyes, and patted Marnie's hand as the doctor took a seat at her desk and clicked around on her screen. "Yes, they can take you right away. Just walk over to Ultrasound. Bea knows the way and they will take you right in. Then come back here and I'll take some time to review the ultrasound with you."

Wrought with confusion, Marnie sat up, straightened out her clothes, the doctor not making direct eye-contact as they exited the exam room and she followed Bea out of the clinic, no words exchanged between the friends, just Bea's supportive hand on her shoulder as they walked to ultrasound.

Everything became a blur after that, like Marnie was outside her body. The ultrasound, the concerned looks, the sadness in Bea's eyes. Dr. Danville telling her that the baby had died in utero, and she would have to be admitted, then induced to deliver it stillborn. The disturbing calm in the delivery room, the kind soothing voice of the nurse that encouraged her to push and solemn look on the doctor's face as she delivered. The pain, the excruciating pain, the barrage of sobs and tears, the tiny bundle carried out of the room as she closed her eyes and prayed that if she slept, she would wake up from this terrible nightmare.

MARNIE WOKE with her head aching, her body feeling like she had done battle. Her eyes peeling open slowly, the cloudy silhouettes of faces watching her coming into focus. She saw her Madre first, her eyes wet with tears as she took Marnie's hand, giving it a supportive squeeze. Next, she saw her Padre, Abuela, and Bea were there too. She looked at Bea, whose face was red and eyes puffy, her mouth in a grim line. Marnie scanned everyone in the room with pure sorrow and concern on all their faces, and her chin trembled as tears filled her eyes again.

"Oh Mila." her mother whispered, her voice shaking with emotion. "We know, and we are so sorry."

With that, the entire sequence of events flooded back, threatening to drown her as a flood of tears burst forth, the realization of what she had been through finally registering in her brain. Multiple sets of arms wrapped around her as she sobbed, and only the voice of her Abuela sending out a prayer in Spanish could be heard over her anguished cries.

CHAPTER 7

A year and a half ago - New Year's Eve:

When Marnie invited Davis to join her and some friends to go listen to her brother's band play at a local Honky Tonk Bar in St. Augustine, Davis accepted immediately. He had two more nights here in Primrose, and all he wanted was to spend them with Marnie. Plus, the prospect of a New Year's kiss was far too much for him to pass on.

Freshly showered, he slipped into a pair of dark wash jeans he knew Marnie liked from the way he caught her checking him out. Adding an olive-colored T-shirt that stretched over his muscular chest and showed off his impressive biceps, he pulled on a pair of brown cowboy boots he fished out of the back of his closet. Ready for his first New Years Eve celebration in years, he exited his bedroom, slowing at Marnie's bedroom door where Lover by Taylor Swift wafted through from inside, and Marnie's sweet voice could be heard singing along. Davis smiled, making his way to the kitchen where he retrieved his phone from his pocket and leaned on the kitchen counter, swiping it open and seeing a message from Bea asking him to come over tomorrow, his last full day in Primrose. Davis felt guilty not spending as much time with his sister as he had promised, but she too was preoccupied with her new relationship with Garrett, so neither seemed to notice. Hearing a door open and close in the hallway, he stood up straight and tucked the phone into his pocket. Marnie rounded the cased opening and his jaw slacked, all breath escaping from his lungs. She was wearing a dark wash form fitted jean dress that hugged every curve perfectly. The top was unbuttoned just enough to take in the swell of her breasts and the short length showed off beautiful, strong legs. Brown knee length cowboy boots finished the outfit. Her shoulder length hair was down, in bouncy waves, her face was made up to extenuate her beautiful eyes, smoky and sultry. *She looks like a goddess.* Without a second thought, Davis rounded the peninsula and strode over to her, setting his hand on her waist as he pulled her into him, wanting nothing more than to feel the heat of her body against his. Her hands braced on his chest; her eyes transfixed on his as they both stood there, a moment of passion passing between them. This was the first time since their kiss in the hallway that Davis had drawn her close, and the surge of attraction between them was palpable. Cutting the sexual tension, he rasped out, "You look incredible."

A smile tugged at Marnie's lips as she glanced down at

herself and then let her eyes roam over him daringly as she replied. "And you look edible."

His pulse quickened with her comment and immediately very dirty thoughts crossed his mind as his groin tightened painfully. *God, I want her.* Before he could give into his desires and lean in to capture her lips, she stepped away from his hold. She turned and made her way to the front entrance, where she reached for her jacket.

"Please allow me," Davis said, putting out his hand. Marnie smiled sweetly, handing him her jacket, and turning. The sweet sugar scent of her perfume capturing his senses and making his head swirl. Helping her into her sleeves, he settled the coat on her shoulders, leaned in and brushed her hair to the side. Marnie sucked in a breath as she turned her face slightly and cleared her throat, breaking them from the intimate moment. "We better get going," Davis said, huskily reaching for his jacket.

Marnie nodded; her gaze focused forward as they left the house with Davis's heart hammering in his chest as he followed her out the door.

* * *

THE DRIVE to the bar was relatively quiet, Marnie's thoughts going a mile a minute as she replayed the soft brush of his fingertips on her skin as he moved her hair to the side. The feel of his powerful body behind her and the heat of his breath on her neck as he leaned in dizzying her mind. *Protect your heart. He's leaving in two days,* her internal voice kept telling her, but she didn't want to listen. The more time she spent with Davis, the more she wanted him.

Driving up to the Pickled Pig, Davis laughed, taking in the cheesy neon sign, a winking pig with a cowboy hat.

"Awesome, right?" Marnie asked, opening her door, and exiting the car.

Davis quickly rounded the vehicle and put out his hand to her. She glanced down at his open palm and back to his questioning eyes. A smile tugged at her lips as she took his offered hand, threading her fingers with his. Looking down at their joined hands, she cocked an eyebrow at him in question. "What's this?"

"A possibility," he replied, giving her a coltish grin.

With a nod and a wide smile painting her lips, she squeezed his hand as they walked into the bar together.

* * *

DAVIS HAD BEEN STRUNG TIGHT all night. Marnie danced, the luscious lines of her curvaceous body moving rhythmically to the music, and he was transfixed, his eyes never leaving her. Davis self-admittedly was not much of a dancer, but when Marnie pulled him onto the floor for a salsa inspired song, he wanted nothing more than to dance with this stunning woman just to feel the headiness of having her close. The way she moved with such fluidity was so sexy and sensual. He was sure his mouth had gone dry just taking it all in. Putting her hands on his hips, she encouraged him to move to the rhythm and giggled when he struggled to capture the tempo. He didn't care if he looked like an idiot as she had her hands on him and that alone made any humiliation worth it. The music slowed; the crowd paired up as her brother Rami went into a set of slow sultry ballads. Glancing up at him, Marnie drew him in with her chocolate brown eyes silently asking him to dance with her. The countdown turned to 5 minutes before the New Year, and he wasn't going to let this opportunity go. Pulling her in, her body pressed against his, the intense heat between seemed ready to ignite. They swayed to the music, their bodies finding the rhythm of the music, the beat of their hearts part of the soundtrack. The music stopped and Rami took to the mic as everyone counted down to the new year. 10, 9, 8, 7, 6, 5, 4, 3, 2, 1… Happy New Years! The bar exploded as Auld Lang Syne played. Around them friends hugged, and couples embraced with passionate kisses. Davis's eyes met Marnie's, sparkling with something in their depths that he hadn't yet seen. *Desire.*

"Davis." Marnie breathed out. "Kiss me, please."

Davis furrowed his brow and looked deep into her eyes. "If I kiss you, I'm going to want so much more, Marnie."

"Then take more. I want it too," she confessed, her words coming out husky and breathless.

Davis smiled, drawing her closer, his tongue darting out to wet his lips as he feathered his hands in her hair. She lifted her chin to him, their breaths mingling hot and heady. Her tantalizing breath smelled like lime and tequila, as he was overcome with the need to taste her lips. Lowering his head, she closed her eyes as he brushed his lips to hers, gentle and sweet, relishing the pillowy softness of her lips against his. When her tongue darted out, teasing his upper lip, he met her, their mouths opening as their kiss deepened and their tongues danced. There was nothing restraining or respectful about this kiss. It was raw and needy, a foreshadow of where the night could take them. They kissed like they were dying of thirst and only they could quench each other. His hands roamed over her back, over the curve at her waist and back up to tangle in her hair. Davis wanted her. Needed her, and he was done holding back.

* * *

MARNIE'S HEART thrummed in her chest as they drove back to Primrose, Davis's hand laced with hers. She had never felt so anxious in her life, glancing over at the gorgeous man next to her she wanted more than anything in this moment. The decision had been made in her mind and she wanted to give Davis all of her, a gift before he left. Having spent so much time with him over the past 12 days, her body craved to feel that ultimate closeness with him, a man she desired fully and knew she was starting to feel real feelings for. As they pulled into the driveway, Davis exited the car and came around to the passenger side, opening the door. Climbing out of the vehicle, his hand reached for hers, lacing their fingers. Davis smiled sweetly at her, and she internally melted, knowing that once they entered that house, all restraint would be gone.

Unlocking the door, Davis hung up the car keys and took off his jacket. Marnie followed, nervous and unsure of how this was going to go. They both pulled off their cowboy boots, him struggling to get one off, eliciting a little giggle from her. No words passing between them. He took her hand, guiding her down the hallway to the bedrooms. Glancing from his door to hers, he raised an eyebrow in question and met her gaze.

"My room." she whispered, her voice coming out raspy with need.

They entered her room, and he shut the door gently. Marnie turned her back to the bed, facing him, their eyes locked, intense, and hungry. He approached her slowly and she could swear she could hear the loud thumping of her heart in the quiet room. Reaching for her, he gripped her waist, bringing her flush with his body, and ran his hands up her back. She braced herself, hands splayed on his chest as she looked up at him, his eyes dark with desire.

"We don't have to do this, if you don't want to," he said, giving her an out.

She shook her head as she panted out, "No, I want this. I want you to be my first."

Davis stopped, his hands halting their caress as he brought his hand up and cupped her face, his green eyes searching hers as he asked. "Are you a virgin?"

She nodded. "You'll be my first." She replied, her eyes falling to her feet, now feeling insecure about her confession. "I just wanted it to go to someone special."

Davis slowly lifted her chin to meet his sincere gaze as she said with conviction. "I'm honored that you've chosen me."

Emotion caught in her throat from his sweet words. Before tears could escape, he lowered his lips to hers in a dove-like kiss so unimaginably tender it made her heart sing.

Bringing his other hand to her face, he whispered against her lips. "I promise to take care of you."

Marnie wasn't sure if it was a promise for tonight or for forever, but she wasn't about to ask. *This is happening.* Davis guided her over to the bed and reached over his head to pull off his T-shirt. She took him in, his powerful upper body glistening in the faint moonlight cascading through her bedroom window. Tracing her fingers over his tattoo, she lifted her eyes to him, bringing her fingertips over his jawline and down to the dip in his chin. He closed his eyes for a moment, as if savoring the feel of her touch. Opening his eyes, he looked down to her dress and slowly started unbuttoning the front, her navy satin bra coming into view. He licked his lips at the sight of her large breasts barely contained by the soft fabric as he slipped the top of the dress over her shoulders and down her arms, letting the fabric fall to her waist. He ran his hands over her shoulders and leaned in, kissing the side of her neck, making a trail with his tongue over to her ear, rolling it between his lips. She let out a moan of approval as she reached down to slide the rest of the dress over her hips, letting it fall to the floor at her feet. He stepped back, his eyes roaming over her body, and he smiled a coquettish smile of approval.

"Do you even realize how sexy you are?" he asked, stepping back into her space, his hands now running up the side of her body over the sides of her breasts.

She shivered as he reached behind her and unclasped her bra, sliding it over her arms and off. Taking in her full breasts, peaked and heavy, Davis lowered his face, taking a rosy peak in his mouth and caressing it with his tongue. She closed her eyes, the sensation intense and going straight to her pulsating core. She reached for the belt of his jeans, her hands shaking with both nervousness and desire, slowly undoing his belt buckle as he continued to lavish her breasts with his lips and tongue. He looked up from his ministrations as she went to the button of his jeans, and he stopped her, grabbing her hand. Surprised, her eyes darted up, meeting his hungry gaze.

"Let me," he offered, sliding his jeans over his behind and down his muscular thighs, exposing his black boxer briefs. Pulling his jeans all the way off, he kicked them away and faced her. This was the most undressed she had seen him, and she couldn't help but take in his thick cinched waist, the deep cut of the v at his hips and his powerful tree trunk thighs. Desire heightened as her eyes roamed over the thick ridge of his manhood behind his boxers. Looking up at him, knowing he saw her eyes dilate as she took him in. He pulled her close, his large hands threading through her hair at the back of her neck and bringing her lips to his in a deep, sensual kiss. Pulling away ever so slightly, he whispered against her mouth. "Lay down on the bed, sugar."

Marnie complied, laying back on the bed, as his powerful body stood over her, the richness of his green eyes glinting in the faint light of the room.

"I need to taste you," he confessed, as he lowered himself to his knees and hooked his fingers into the sides of her panties. Lifting her behind off the bed to help him, he slid them down her legs, kissing a path along her inner thigh. The rough scratch of his stubble made goosebumps form on her skin as he ran his large hands over her inner thighs, spreading her open to him. She lifted her head and met his lustful gaze, as he lowered his head between her legs and kissed her center. Her breath caught as he took one languid sweep through her folds, causing her to grow wetter with each lap and flick of his tongue against her pulse point. Setting a steady rhythm, lapping, kissing, sucking, causing erotic whimpers and long-drawn-out moans to fall from her lips. Marnie was lost. Lost to all the new sensations he was eliciting as he brought her closer to the edge.

"Davis, oh my God." she cried out as he continued to consume her, hungrily eating her arousal, and causing her to vibrate with need. Marnie bowed her back off the bed as she unapologetically rocked into his mouth, creating more delicious friction. Reading her body and knowing she was getting close, he brought the bundle of nerves at her center between his lips and sucked, making her gasp in pleasure as he tipped her over the edge. Closing her eyes, an exquisite warmth took over her body, and she moaned out loud, her core pulsating as she let go. He continued his attention until she came down, little aftershocks of her release surging through her. She lay there satiated for a moment, unable to speak, reveling in a post orgasm haze. Suddenly feeling cold, Marnie shivered, and she opened her eyes, expecting to see Davis's handsome face above her. But when she opened her eyes, he wasn't there. He was gone. Shocked, she sat up, glancing around the room, but she was alone, almost as if what just happened was a figment of her imagination or a dream that she had woken from. Reaching for the covers, she pulled them up to cover her nakedness, her room feeling cold and empty as her inner voice repeated. *You're alone. He's gone.*

* * *

SEARCHING THROUGH HIS BEDSIDE TABLE, Davis finally found what he was looking for, a box of condoms he bought years before. Breathing a sigh of relief, he fished one out of the box and made his way back to Marnie's room to find her sitting on the bed, her knees up and head resting on the top of her knees, a comforter covering her beautiful body. She raised her head, her eyes glossy and shining in the dimly lit room. His face fell instantly as he took in her stoney expression and noticed her body language as she clutched tightly to the comforter covering her naked body. *She's upset.* He approached the bed slowly, condom in his palm, as he sat down on the edge of the bed and reached for her hand. She pulled her hand away, turning her head as she wiped at a tear that escaped down her cheek. Confusion clouded his thoughts. *Did I do something wrong? Did I hurt her? What did I do?*

"Are you okay, Sugar?" he asked, trying to meet her gaze.

She was quiet and he could see her trying to steady her emotions as she slowly turned her head, her eyes falling to her hands as she whispered, "Davis, I think you should go."

"I am so sorry, I needed to go get..." he started until she interrupted him.

"You vanished!" she exclaimed, raising her gaze to meet his, a mix of anger and disappointment in their depths. "How do you think that made me feel?" she asked, her voice breaking with her question. "I let you do that to me, and you left."

"I, Marnie, I…" he tried, but she held up her hand.

"Just like you're going to leave in two days." she added, her voice quiet and resolute.

Confused by this sudden turn of events, Davis growled out. "That's not fair, Marnie, I have no choice. I have to return to my job."

"And I would have been another conquest, which, months from now, would be a distant memory." She commented, her words harsh and biting.

He rose from the bed, frustration overtaking him, feeling so misunderstood at this moment. "I'm not like that," he said, his voice low and flat. "I don't treat women that way."

She met his frustrated gaze, her brown eyes flat and guarded as she said. "I don't know that, because I don't know you."

Davis felt like he had been slapped, the sting of her words breaking his heart. *What have I been doing these past two weeks? I've shared more about myself than I have with any other woman.* A painful lump of emotion constricted his throat, and he swallowed down hard. *I can't let her see how much her words hurt me.* Holding his head up high, he made his way to her door, taking one last glance at the woman he was falling for and, at her request, left the room.

* * *

DAVIS RAN his hands through his hair for what felt like the millionth time since New Year's Day. Today he was leaving, needing to catch his first flight at 5 p.m. Marnie hadn't talked to him since she kicked him out of her room and asked him to leave. He was so angry and disappointed that she wouldn't at the very least let him explain, but as he lay in bed awake till the early hours of dawn, he realized why she was so hurt. She felt rejected. He had given her pleasure and disappeared. Albeit for good reason, he was gone too long, and it made her feel abandoned at that vulnerable moment. A moment she had never experienced before with any other man and rather than kissing her, holding her, and telling her how beautiful she was when she came undone, he left like an insensitive, selfish idiot. Now the woman he was falling in love with wouldn't speak to him. Marnie completely icing him out.

Feeling the thick tension in the house, he spent New Year's Day with Bea, Garrett and Amelia and was thankful for the distraction. When he returned to the house later that evening, Marnie's vehicle was gone, and she hadn't come home for the night. Not sure if he would see her again, he walked down to the Eazy that morning, picked her up some flowers and put them in a vase for her on the kitchen table. It wasn't much, but it was something. A peace offering, if nothing else. With his ride coming shortly to pick him up, his uniform on, his duffle bag packed and waiting at the door, and he had just enough time to write her a note. Finding paper in the drawer, he began to write:

Dear Marnie,

I have so much I want to say to you, and I wish I had the

opportunity to say it to you in person instead of writing it here in this note. But since that's not going to happen, I guess here goes. Marnie Perez, you are incredible. I've never met anyone so kind, selfless, and beautiful inside and out. I appreciate all of you, even when you're upset with me, like you are now. And I want you to know that I think you are perfect, simply perfect in every way. I will miss you.

Love Davis

A car horn sounded outside, signaling his ride was waiting. With a resolute sigh, he propped the notecard against the vase of flowers, picked up his duffle bag and slung it over his shoulder, then left through the front door with a heavy heart, unsure of when he would return or if he would ever see Marnie again.

CHAPTER 8

Marnie sat on the front porch, staring out onto her quiet street. It was a chilly day and sparkling frost lingered on the trees and bushes surrounding the porch. She bundled herself in a thick quilt as she sat there trembling from both the cold and her grief, her eyes red and raw and her mind in an exhausted fog. It has been three weeks since she lost the baby, the baby she didn't know she wanted. After Marnie was discharged, her family, as was tradition, held a memorial honoring the loss and asking their ancestors to watch over the baby. She liked to think it was a little boy. At least that was what she had in her head all along. Davis Jr. or DJ as she referred to him. A name honoring his father. *Davis.* She hadn't talked to him yet but gave Bea permission to inform him about their loss. She simply didn't have the strength to share the sad news as she mourned. As she expected he had emailed, she got the notifications on her phone, but she couldn't open them. Just seeing his name made her want to cry, and she was so exhausted by all the crying. *The proposal.* Just the day before all this happened, he had proposed and given her his grandmother's ring. She held up her hand letting the stones catch a hint of light. It was such a beautiful ring and carried deep sentimental meaning to the Baxter family. She needed to give it back to Davis. *Surely, he doesn't want to marry me now.* Marnie's heart ached, as tears brimmed in her eyes, and she wrapped the quilt tighter around her shoulders. Her only protection from the rest of the world.

* * *

DAVIS WAS beside himself with worry. It had been two months since he had proposed to Marnie on video and two months since she gave birth to their stillborn baby. Bea had contacted him with the terrible news as she had been with Marnie through the entire ordeal. He wanted nothing more than to talk to Marnie, but Bea urged him to give her time saying she was struggling with the loss. If space was what Marnie needed, he would give it to her. But the unfathomable thought of what she had been through caused the pain of their mutual loss to sit heavy on his chest and when he was alone, the tears of mourning fell. Now two months later, after reaching out countless times with not so much as a word back from her, he didn't know if she wanted to see him ever again. *Are we still engaged, or does she want to call it off?* He had no idea, and this radio silence was killing him. Garrett had let him know that she had returned to work, her bakery having been kept open with the help of her supportive family and a baking assistant she had hired. That was good at least. As soon as he got the devastating news, he applied for leave but was turned down and told he couldn't apply for another six months. Given the possibility of only getting leave next summer at the earliest. The waiting was brutal, but he needed to try one more time. Maybe one more email would get through to her.

Email from Sergeant Davis Baxter, Canadian Armed Forces – UN Peacekeepers to Marnie Perez @ Everything you Knead:

Marnie,

I've reached out to you so many times, I've lost count. I figured I would try one more time, to get through to you. I need to talk to you so badly, Marnie, it hurts. I think about what you went through and the thought of not being there with you, helping you through it is literally tearing me apart. I should have been by your side. I'll only get leave next summer at the earliest so please know, I've done everything I'm able to do, to get to you. When I'm finally able to come back to Primrose, I want to see you, I want to spend time with you, just stare into those beautiful brown eyes and wrap my arms around you. I dream about holding you every night. Just holding you, Sugar. Thoughts of you consume me. I still want to marry you, Marnie. Please reply. I miss you.

In my thoughts always,
Davis

Marnie stared at her computer screen, her bottom lip

between her teeth, her chin trembling as she wiped at the tears that streaked her face. This was Davis's 27th email in the past two months and she hadn't responded to any of them. Having only opened the first one two weeks ago, she went through them one by one, taking in his words, his pleas for her to respond, his concerns, his regrets, how he thinks of her and how he still wants her. Yet not a single email said he loved her. *How could he marry me, now if he doesn't love me?* There was nothing binding them together now and although she was very much aware of how she was falling in love with Davis, she told herself she would be okay. She was confident she could move on, eventually. She just needed to make a clean break and hope her feelings would diminish with time and space. Taking a deep breath, she started typing her reply:

Email from Marnie Perez @ Everything you Knead to Sergeant Davis Baxter, Canadian Armed Forces – UN Peacekeepers:

Davis,

The past few months have been hard, and I understand how you couldn't be here. I read all your emails, have taken in your words and with careful consideration I don't think I can marry you, Davis. When you come back to Primrose, I'll return your grandmother's ring. I'll also be looking for a new place to live this spring. Don't worry about me, please. I'll be okay. Stay safe.

Marnie

Davis stared at Marnie's email a long time, reading it repeatedly. He buried his head in his hands in frustration.

She was shutting him out again. It couldn't be over between them as it hadn't even begun. He could understand her wanting to call off the engagement, but he wasn't going to let her go altogether. He wanted to be with her, and he knew in his heart she wanted to be with him too.

* * *

BEA AND GARRETT'S Wedding Day:

Marnie's traitorous eyes drifted over to Davis pacing the front entrance of the church waiting for his sister. He looked so incredibly sexy in his tailored suit, and she couldn't help but check him out. He had arrived five days ago, just in time for pre wedding festivities to begin and would be leaving in two days, his leave short this time around. For Bea's sake, Marnie was grateful he was able to be here and walk Bea down the aisle. It would be a sweet moment. Davis glanced up and offered her a reluctant smile, his emerald eyes meeting her across the entrance. She smiled back, her thoughts immediately going to how much she missed his handsome face. The awkwardness and disappointment of the last time she saw him had faded with time.

"Hi Marnie." he said quietly, across the space between them as he raised his hand with a wave.

With this being the first time they had seen each other in a year and a half, she had spent countless hours stewing on what happened and now with time and space felt guilty about how they'd left things. She'd been hurt, reactionary in the moment and had said things she was sure had hurt him.

"Hi Davis." she replied, meeting his gaze. "You look nice."

He looked down at his suit and smiled back at her, then letting his eyes survey her head to toe, he replied, "You look beautiful."

The familiar heat of a blush crept up her face and settled in her cheeks. *What is it about his compliments that always get to me?* "Thank you." she replied. "Do you think after the wedding, can could talk?"

"I would like that. I have so..." he began before they were interrupted by Savanah who was instructing everyone to enter the front entrance and line up for the wedding to begin. Davis glanced at Marnie, a look shared between them, to continue their conversation later.

DAVIS SAT in the front pew watching his older sister say her vows to the love of her life. As she promised to love Garrett forever, he found himself glancing over to Marnie. She was so gorgeous in her dark pink bridesmaid dress, her dark brown wavy hair pulled back at the sides letting tendrils fall against her face. That beautiful face with her large chocolate brown eyes, so emotional and shining with tears of happiness for her friend. Simply looking at her stirred so much emotion within him. He felt his chest tighten painfully as he swallowed down hard. He had missed her over the past year and a half. Having left, without closure, without confirmation as to why she had shut him out. Leaving him to try to piece the puzzle together himself. The more he went through the memory of that night, he was sure he knew why she did it, but her explosive reaction still perplexed him. He wasn't given a chance to explain, but rather was told that all his efforts to get to know her better and to pursue her affections were in vain. It was hard to hear at the time, but now as he looked at her, radiantly standing beside his sister, so much time had passed since that confusing night, he was sure that their story wasn't over. Their story was only just beginning.

* * *

MARNIE KEPT STEALING glances at Davis throughout the wedding ceremony and could feel his intense gaze on her as well. The way he looked at her stirred feelings she had tried so hard to tamper down. He had a way about him, a way he made her feel desired and beautiful. They needed to talk, and she needed to apologize.

After the wedding, pictures were taken. The wedding party and family lingered as different shots were posed, and everyone waited to be directed accordingly. Marnie's senses were awakened by the spicy, musky scent of his cologne, before she noticed him standing beside her. *God, he smells so good.* She met his gaze, his hands casually in his pockets as he rocked back and forth in his dress shoes, waiting next to her. She glanced at him, offering a tentative smile as she commented, "It was a beautiful wedding."

"It was," he replied, looking fondly towards his sister

and Garrett as they posed for a picture. "I'm so happy for Bea. She has found her happily ever after."

Marnie followed his gaze to Bea, a smile tugging at her lips as she took in his sweet words and added, "It's not easy to find."

"It's not, but I think if you find it, you need to hold on to it," he declared, his gaze shifting over to her. "At least I would."

She turned her eyes to meet his, the conviction in his gaze going straight to her heart.

"Davis!" Bea exclaimed. "I want to get a few pictures of the two of us."

"Sounds good Bea." he replied. Davis put his large warm hand on the small of Marnie's back and a jolt of electricity in his touch sizzled through her body. That familiar feeling of longing resurfacing as she met his eyes. "We'll talk after dinner," he whispered just so she could hear him. "I have a lot I want to say."

Marnie watched as he strode over to his sister, gave her a big hug, and got into place for the photographer. His eyes darted to her momentarily, a promise that they would indeed talk later tonight.

* * *

THE RECEPTION WAS HELD at Prairie Sky Acres in a large tent on the front lawn. Round tables adorned with light pink tablecloths and beautiful floral centerpieces framed a large wooden dance floor built by Hayden Hastings. Delicate tulle and sparkly fairy lights draped the ceiling of the tent as the sun set across the prairie. Dinner was delicious, speeches had been made, and the couple had just had their first dance. Marnie felt tingly and light, taking it all in. She couldn't help but fantasize about her wedding someday. What she would want, who she would want to be there, her mind drifting off in a daydream as she was caught up in the love and bliss of this magical day. She glanced over to Davis, who caught her gaze and gestured with his head for her to meet him outside the tent.

Swallowing back her nervousness, she excused herself from the table and followed him as he made his way to the front steps of the farmhouse where they could talk privately. Taking a seat, she sat down next to him, offering him a timid smile. Neither spoke for a moment, an awkwardness still looming between them. Breaking the silence, both spoke, blurting out in unison. "I'm sorry." Davis and Marnie both started laughing and Davis shook his head, gesturing to her.

"Ladies, first."

Marnie looked down at her hands for a moment, trying to formulate the right words. "Davis, I'm so sorry for how I reacted that night, the night we…" she gestured, rolling her hands. "The night, you, you know… seriously Davis, this is harder than I thought it would be."

Davis chuckled lightly and reached for her hand, threading his fingers with hers. "It's okay, Marnie. I remember that night. I remember it well," he said, giving her a wink.

Marne felt the blush start as she continued. "Well, after you, you know, satisfied me and I thought you would be my first, you were suddenly gone and I got in my head, thinking maybe you didn't enjoy it, or maybe you were running for the hills or maybe you thought you had made a mistake."

He squeezed her hand, his brows furrowing, encouraging her to finish.

"I thought maybe you didn't find me attractive and then I started thinking about you leaving so soon and how I was about to give you all of me and then never see you again," she confessed. "I overreacted and looking back, I feel guilty for what I said to you. I need you to know all our conversations and time spent together meant the world to me. You opened up to me and let me in and I know it's not something you find easy to do. I felt close to you and trusted you. I trusted you enough to want to give you a part of me I had never given anyone else. I guess I just wanted to say I'm sorry for overreacting, and I wish that night went differently."

He looked up at her, emotion in his eyes, and he offered her a smile as he replied. "I accept your apology and I appreciate it." Looking down at his hands for a moment, he brought his gaze back to hers as he said, "I want to say I'm sorry as well and don't regret anything that happened between us. I know, I played a huge part in the entire trajectory of that night. I made a lot of mistakes which, in retrospect, I should've realized would have come across as insensitive. First of all, leaving the room after I pleasured you was stupid. You hadn't even had a chance to process what had just happened and here I go, leaving the room to find protection. I knew what I was thinking at that moment, and all I was thinking about was myself. You were about to give me a part of you that was sacred, and I was an eager idiot. I wanted to experience it with you, so at that moment all I was thinking about was the act, not the feelings around the act. I should have stayed with you, told you how beautiful it was to see you come apart and then if you still wanted to give me more, sought what I needed to keep us both safe."

"I appreciate how you thought of that, though. That's the thing. Looking back my reaction was so impulsive and just me feeling insecure in that moment." she added.

"You know you have nothing to feel insecure about, right?" he asked, kissing the back of hand. "Marnie you are literally the most beautiful, sexiest woman I have ever laid eyes on."

Marnie felt her heart flutter with his compliments, and she looked down.

He reached over, lifting her chin to meet his eyes. "I'm being serious, Marnie. I still desire you as much as I did that night. I still want to make love to you."

Marnie took in his words, searching his eyes for sincerity. In his eyes she saw that, and so much more. A deep longing, an intense hunger for her.

"If you can trust me again, I want to give you the night you deserve to have."

Before she could answer or reject him, he leaned in and tenderly brushed his lips over hers. With the sweet touch of his lips her entire body exhaled the breath she had held so long. He was gentle, reverent, and his lips felt so excruciatingly good. She wanted to, oh, how she wanted to give in. They broke their kiss and Davis pulled her into him, the warmth of his body soothing her very soul. He felt so good. It made tears burn her eyes, and she sighed. The sound of shoes clicking on the walkway sounded and they released their embrace to see Ever Hastings a few feet away.

"There you two are!" Ever exclaimed. "They're about to cut the cake!"

"We better go." Marnie said quietly, pushing the emotion of the moment down as she got up from the step and brushed the dust off her dress. "We can't miss the cake."

CHAPTER 9

"Hola, Abuela! Como estas?" Marnie said as she entered her Abuela's home in St. Augustine. Her Abuela had requested her to come early to their weekly family dinner, as she wanted to visit with her before the house filled with family.

"Hola Mila." Abuela replied, giving her a hug and a kiss on the cheek. "Thank you for coming early before your loco brothers show up. This way we can talk privately for a while."

Marnie suspected a talk was coming, as she hadn't yet had a private conversation with Abuela since losing her baby four months ago. She was now mentally ready for a lecture. She sat down at the kitchen table and her Abuela sat down next to her, turning her chair to face her, and taking her hands in hers.

"How are you, Martina?" she asked, her dark brown eyes kind, and imploring.

"I'm okay." Marnie replied. "Work is busy, and I have lots of custom orders to fill this month."

Abuela gave Marnie a chiding look. "I'm not asking about your work. How are you doing, Mila?" Marnie sighed and glanced away, taking a deep breath to steady her emotions. She looked back to her grandmother, her eyes glistening with unshed tears. Abuela's eyes drifted down to her hand, her gaze returning to meet hers as she said, "This is a beautiful ring you are wearing. Is this from Davis?"

Marnie nodded and internally scolded herself for not taking it off yet. She loved the ring so much and although she called off their engagement, somehow, when she wore it, it felt like Davis was with her. Marnie understood it was unhealthy for her to cling onto that, but somehow just having a piece of him comforted her. She knew she should take it off but every time she did, she found herself putting it back on again. Feeling the need to explain, she replied. "Davis asked me to marry him before I lost the baby, and this was his grandmother's ring."

"A family heirloom. Very nice. So, you're engaged then?" Abuela asked, seeking clarification.

"I called it off." Marnie said, looking down at the ring, then back to meet Abuela's confused gaze.

"Oh, I see. Because of losing the baby?"

Marnie nodded. Her grandmother held her hands for a moment, taking the time to formulate her words before she spoke. "Sometimes life has a strange way of bringing us down a path we least expect and sometimes we are faced with challenges that seem too hard to overcome. Everything that happens to us is part of a plan and everyone we meet is part of that plan as well. We're meant to meet certain people, to share experiences both good and bad. Those shared experiences can either bring us closer or tear us apart, but we can choose which one it will be." Marnie stared into the wise eyes of her Abuela as she continued. "I like Davis. He is a good man with a pure heart. I felt that the first time you brought him here to meet us. I also could see the way he looks at you, Mila. He looks at you like a man that has never seen anything more beautiful. Maybe he hasn't fully realized it yet, but he loves you. I could see it in his eyes. I truly believe he wouldn't have given you this ring if he didn't want to marry you."

"But Abuela, he only proposed because of the baby. The situation forced him into it." Marnie protested.

"Like I said, life has strange ways sometimes." She repeated, squeezing Marnie's hand. "You two have shared a great loss and you need to hold on to each other tighter, not push each other away."

"He said he still wanted to marry me." Marnie confessed, looking down at the ring on her finger.

"And what did you say?" Abuela asked, meeting Marnie's gaze.

"I told him we were done and that I would be looking for a new place to live."

Abuela shook her head and said, "Well then Mila, you need to fix that. A good man like Davis doesn't come around every day. You need to open your heart and to give him a chance to show you how much he loves you."

MARNIE REPEATED ABUELA'S WORDS, over and over in her head. *Did I create a narrative that wasn't there?* When she told Davis it was over, she was certain that he was just looking for an excuse to call it off. *Maybe I was wrong. Maybe I was too hasty.* It was time to talk to Bea and ask for her insight. She needed to know if there was still a chance he wanted her in his life.

Marnie sat in the booth at the Eazy waiting for Bea to arrive. She was nervous and kept fidgeting with the bottom button of her blouse. The door chime sounded, and she looked up to see the brilliant red curls of her dear friend. Bea waved and made her way to the booth at the back of the café. Marnie picked it away from the prying ears of locals with the hope of a private conversation.

"Hey, thanks for meeting me," Marnie said as Bea slid into the booth.

"Sure. How've you been?" Bea asked as she settled in and met her with a compassionate gaze.

"Feeling a lot better." Bea nodded and offered her a half smile. An unusually awkward silence falling on the friends. The waitress came and took their orders and once they had their drinks, Marnie broke the ice that seemed to have formed around them. "First of all, Bea, I can't tell you how much I appreciate you being there for me these past five months." Marnie said, giving Bea a warm smile. "Your friendship has meant everything to me."

Bea smiled and looked down, almost contemplative, then replied, "I'm going to just cut to the chase, Marnie and please forgive me in advance for being so straight forward. I know you've been through so much these past five months and honestly, I completely understand shutting down and not wanting to talk about it. I can understand you wanting time to process and to mourn, but I know you're in a better place now and have started talking about what happened to you. Which I think is great. It's part of the healing process. However, the only person you haven't talked to about what happened is Davis. He might not have been physically present when everything went down, but he lost something very precious that day, too." Marnie swallowed down hard, feeling her words and emotions rise in her throat as Bea continued, "Davis lost that baby, too. He was excited about it. Excited about becoming a father. He was so excited about marrying you and starting a life with you and your child. And now, Marnie, he is devastated."

Devastated? Marnie's eyes grew wide as she took in her friend's words. A wave of emotion slapping her straight in the face. With tears in her eyes and a trembling whisper, she asked, "How do I fix this?"

"For starters, you email him back." Bea replied, matter of fact. "And you listen to him. Marnie, he may have not given you validation yet in the form of an 'I love you', but I know my brother and it's coming. I can see how he feels for you when he looks at you. You just need to let him in and be patient."

Email from Marnie Perez @ Everything you Knead to Sergeant Davis Baxter, Canadian Armed Forces – UN Peacekeepers:
Davis,
This email may seem like it's out of the blue, and yes, I suppose

it is, but I want to start by saying, 'I'm sorry'. So sorry I ended things even before they began. I've done so much soul searching in the past few months and have spoken to my Abuela (by the way she is a big Davis fan) and to your sister, and I realized that I never gave you a chance to talk through our loss. And regrettably, I never listened. I should have taken into consideration your thoughts and feelings about losing our baby and the fact that I didn't was selfish of me. I can't tell you enough how sorry I am, Davis. I hope you can forgive me, and we can start talking again. It doesn't matter what we talk about, I just want and need to talk to you and know you're still there.
Love, Marnie

Email from Sergeant Davis Baxter, Canadian Armed Forces – UN Peacekeepers to Marnie Perez @ Everything you Knead:
Marnie,
I'm not going to lie to you and say you didn't hurt me by breaking things off. It stung me and I spent a few weeks wallowing in self-pity. But mostly I spent my time worried about you. Any sadness and emotions I have regarding our loss are nothing compared to what you went through. That being said, I think you already know, I don't give up that easily when it comes to you. I've been waiting for you, thinking about you, and wanting to talk to you, too. So, let's start over, and press the proverbial reset button. Hi, I'm Sergeant Davis Baxter, and I'm looking for a beautiful, spicy Latina woman who keeps me on my toes and makes me work hard for her affections. Oh, and if she bakes a mean Mexican Chocolate Cake that would be a bonus. Do you know anyone like that?
Anxious for your reply,

Davis

PS I am a big fan of your Abuela as well. Give her a kiss from me.

Email from Marnie Perez @ Everything you Knead to Sergeant Davis Baxter, Canadian Armed Forces – UN Peacekeepers:

Davis,

I think I may know someone that fits that description. It feels good to talk to you again and know you're not angry with me. I would like to try this again. Maybe this time in a little less of a Telenovela fashion. But yes, if you were here, I would like it if you asked me out. We could go out on some dates and perhaps you would romance me a little. Start out with some wooing before the smolder, rather than the other way around this time. Not that I don't like the smolder, especially your brand of smolder. Just a little wooing first next time.

Your feisty Latina,

Marnie

Email from Sergeant Davis Baxter, Canadian Armed Forces – UN Peacekeepers to Marnie Perez @ Everything you Knead:

Marnie,

So, I looked up woo, in the dictionary and the definition is to seek affection or love from someone, usually a woman. As for the smolder, it is defined as to exist or continue in a suppressed state. With that knowledge, I'm all in on wooing you. No more smolder. I don't want to hold back or suppress how I feel about you, Marnie. I want to see you and show you how much I care. I want to say so much to you, but I don't want to email you

how I feel. I want to tell you face to face, in person. I need to look into your beautiful eyes when I do. As for when this wooing can officially begin, I want you to know that I just applied for a 1 month leave and it looks like I should be able to get time off in August. Will you still be in the house? Bea said you decided not to rent out the second room. Will you keep it open for me?
Ready to romance you,
Davis

Email from Marnie Perez @ Everything you Knead to Sergeant Davis Baxter, Canadian Armed Forces – UN Peacekeepers:

Dearest Davis,
Oh, color me intrigued! I look forward to seeing what you have up your sleeve and as for a place to stay, yes, your room will be free, IF you want to use it. I can't wait till August to see your handsome face. I always wonder what you're doing and if you're safe. I looked up UN Peacekeeper efforts in Africa and it looks scary. So much unrest. I know, though, that you're doing your job and keeping others safe, too. Did I ever tell you I think you're brave? Well, I do. Not everyone can do what you do. It takes a very special person. Oh, now I'm excited, Davis! In 4 months, I will see you again and I will bake that Mexican Chocolate Cake you love so much. I'm pretty sure my Abuela will want to make you her famous tamales too. Get ready to eat, oh so many tamales.
Anxiously awaiting your return,
Love Marnie

Email from Sergeant Davis Baxter, Canadian Armed

Forces – UN Peacekeepers to Marnie Perez @ Everything you Knead:

My sweet Marnie,

You are mean. Now all I can think of is your Abuela's tamales, and your Mexican chocolate cake, and eating them both with you, naked. Sorry if that's a bit too bold, but a guy can dream, right? Anyway, I'll be going on a special mission and will be gone for at least 4 weeks with no access to email. I promise this is routine and I'll be safe. When I get back it will be only 3 months until I'm in Primrose, with you. I can't tell you how much these past few months have meant to me, talking to you again. I wish I could see your lovely face, Sugar, but until I can, I will have the memory of you in my heart.

Missing you already,

Davis

CHAPTER 10

The Morning after Bea and Garrett's Wedding

Marnie had no frame of reference for the morning after a night of spectacular sex. In fact, she had no frame of reference for sex at all, but something told her last night was as good as it gets. The way she and Davis came together with such hunger and intensity, it was far more than she expected for her first time. How he worshipped every inch of her, taking his time, making her never feel more beautiful and wanted in her life. How their eyes locked on each other when they finally connected, going slowly, allowing her to adjust to him. She wasn't going to lie. It hurt at first, but Davis was sweet and patient, whispering gentle soothing words in her ear and taking care of her as he promised. The pain morphing to pleasure. She soon found herself enrobed by the exquisite sensations of their bodies moving together.

And when they tumbled into ecstasy, there was no second guessing that she would never and could never regret giving him all of her.

Marnie woke with the wall of warmth behind her, his large hand on her hip possessively. She tried to slip out of the bed, to go to the bathroom, but when she did, he pulled her back into him.

"Davis, I need to pee," she said with a giggle.

He groaned into his pillow and let her go as he watched her walk naked across the room towards the door, a coquettish smile on his face.

She took care of her morning needs and looked down at her naked body, surprised at her confidence around Davis. She had never been this audacious before and would never consider walking around naked. She didn't even like walking around in a bathing suit. But for some reason, the way Davis looked at her with such appreciation in his eyes made her forget all her insecurities. Davis had made it abundantly clear that he liked what he saw, and that fact made her feel daring. She slipped back into the room to find him propped up with one arm, eyes trained on her.

"You are so damn sexy. Do you know that?" he asked, his green eyes flashing with lust.

Marnie smiled, a light blush settling in her cheeks as she strode back to her side of the bed, and he flipped the covers open for her to slide in next to him. When she did, she felt exactly how sexy he thought she was, his hardness pressing against her hip. She turned, her eyes wide, and they both let out a little laugh.

"How are you feeling today?" he asked, resting his hand on her stomach.

"Sore, but good. Really good, actually. Last night was…"

"Incredible." he finished her sentence.

She nodded, turning to face him, and running her fingers over his handsome stubbled face. "I'm happy I gave that part of me to you."

"Thank you," he whispered, his forehead touching hers, their eyes transfixed on each other. "It meant more to me than you know."

Davis bridged the gap between them and brushed his lips to hers with a sweet and reverent kiss. A swell of emotion surfaced as his lips moved with hers, never having experienced this kind of intimacy with another human being. They parted, and she curled around him, burying her head in his hard chest, lazily tracing figure eights through the smattering of red curls there. They lay there a long time, both drifting back to sleep, lost in the ardor of their togetherness.

Hours later a phone rang, waking them both from their peaceful slumber, Davis groaned, peeled himself from Marnie and their cocoon of warmth. Sliding out of bed, he looked around, trying to locate his pants and, finding them, pulled out his phone. "Sargeant Davis Baxter." he answered.

Marnie sat up, pulling the comforter over her bare chest as she listened to him.

"Yes, Sir, thank you Sir. I will make sure to catch that flight." Davis hung up his phone and looked over at Marnie, a look of resignation in his eyes. "I'm being picked up in an hour. My flight has been bumped up and I need to go. I'm so sorry, Marnie. I was hoping we could spend the day together."

Marnie rolled out of bed, walked to the dresser, pulling out a nightshirt and slipped it on. He rushed around the room, collecting his clothes piece by piece, dressing as he went.

"I have just enough time to get to Bea and Garrett's, shower and pack my things," he said out loud, ticking off a mental checklist.

She spotted his tie in the corner and leaned over to pick it up for him. She held it out, and he pulled her into him, his eyes imploring her. "Please don't take this as me running away or abandoning you. Last night was special to me, Marnie, and I want you to know that."

"I know." she replied with a genuine smile. "You have a job to go back to, I get it."

Offering her a somber smile, he captured her lips in a mind-melting kiss, his hands going under the night shirt to grip her bare behind and give it a squeeze. He groaned against her lips, the ache in his voice almost painful as he said, "I've got to go."

She stepped out of his hold, knowing if she didn't, he would never be ready in time.

Davis rushed out of the bedroom and towards the front door, Marnie following behind. He turned, pulled her flush with his body, leaned in, kissed her chastely but passionately and said, "I will miss you, Sugar."

"I will miss you too, Davis." she replied as she watched him bound down the porch and sprint across the street, disappearing inside Bea and Garrett's home. *Would she see him again? Was this the beginning of something?* She had no answers. All she knew for sure was that she was head over heels in love with him.

* * *

SPRING TURNED into a warm June and the dog days of summer were quickly upon them. It was only six weeks until Davis was scheduled to be home, and as each day slowly passed by, the anticipation of seeing him again grew. Marnie went about her days as she usually did, but her thoughts were constantly on Davis, waiting for his next email. The month he was gone this Spring on a special mission was excruciating and when she got the first email upon his return, she felt like she could breathe again. *How do military wives do this repeatedly?* When she wondered this, she would look down at the beautiful ring still adorning her finger. *I could be one of those wives someday.*

The bakery was closed for the day, and Marnie lingered after hours trying to distract herself by finishing a custom birthday cake. She brought her attention to all the details, piping intricate designs as per the customer's request, when she heard the familiar chime of the door opening and closing. She groaned, internally chiding herself for forgetting to lock the door when she turned the CLOSED SIGN around. Quickly washing her hands, she dried them and hustled into the front of the bakery, ready to either help a rogue customer or send them on their way.

"Sorry, we are..." she started, stopping dead in her

tracks, her eyes meeting the magnetic green gaze of Davis Baxter.

"Hi there, Sugar."

Marnie closed her eyes, then opened them slowly, not believing her eyes. The universe seemed to manifest the man she couldn't stop thinking about. He smiled that oh so handsome smile and instantly her pulse quickened, as she slowly came around the counter. This man she cared so deeply for was here, standing in her bakery in uniform, looking like the best dream. She ran into his arms, bridging the gap between them in seconds, wrapping her arms around his middle, feeling tears well up in her eyes. Davis reciprocated, wrapping his strong arms around her, his hand gently stroking her hair. Davis's strong, powerful body felt so good, so real. *He's here. I can't believe he's here.* Big fat tears started to fall, trailing down her cheeks and her body shook as all the pain of the past months came out with a tidal wave of emotion.

"Don't cry," he whispered against her hair, his voice cracking with his words as he brought his hands to her face, staring deeply into her eyes. He lowered his lips to her cheeks, kissing the salty tears from her face. Then he brought his lips to hers, his kiss tender and sweet, his lips so soft and warm. A kiss she craved more than she wanted to admit. A kiss that she desperately needed. Pulling back, he tenderly wiped the tears from her cheeks, and she let out a long-pained exhale. He smiled down at her, his hands still on her face as he brushed her hair from her eyes affectionately.

"How are you here?" she questioned, searching his gaze for answers.

"There was a little change in plans, and I had an opportunity to take my leave earlier, so I jumped on it. I couldn't wait a day longer to see you," he said sweetly, the rich timbre of his voice making her melt in his arms. "I literally flew into Winnipeg about two hours ago, rented a car and drove straight here."

She smiled and buried her head in his chest, inhaling deeply the masculine scent of him and relishing the feel of his embrace. "You must be exhausted. I'm almost done here; do you want to stay and keep me company and then we can go home together?" She asked, pulling away from him.

"That sounds good to me. Should I order some dinner from the Eazy?" he asked. "That way we can just relax tonight."

"Sounds perfect." She replied, taking his hand and leading him around the counter into the kitchen. She gestured for him to grab a stool from the corner and take a seat at the long worktable.

"What are you working on?" he asked, taking a seat in front of her as she rounded the table and surveyed the almost finished cake.

"A custom birthday cake for this weekend. I just have a few more details and I'm done." She replied, picking up her piping bag.

As Marnie tried to curb her jumble of thoughts and emotions and go into her decorating zone, she was very aware of his eyes on her, watching her every move. Davis had a way of not necessarily making her nervous but more making her incredibly self-aware. Like he was studying her, taking notes on how she did things, her movements, her expressions. It was both strange and exhilarating to have that kind of attention on her and in that moment, she realized how much she missed the warm feeling he elicited just by being nearby. Finishing the last detail, she glanced up to meet his mesmerizing green eyes.

"I love watching you work," he mused. "I imagine it's like a painter or a sculptor creating a masterpiece. You kind of go to another place. It's fascinating to watch."

"So, I'm an artist then?" she asked, looking at her confectionary creation and back at Davis.

"I think so," he replied. "You are so good at what you do. Seriously Marnie, you are so talented."

Pride surged through her as she smiled modestly and swiped her hand in the air as if to feign off his compliment. Marnie liked it though; she liked it a lot. Davis saw her and although she was never good at accepting compliments, when Davis delivered them, they went straight to her heart.

* * *

COMING HOME HAD ALWAYS BEEN BITTERSWEET for Davis. On the one hand, it was always good to be home. On the other hand, the knowledge that he must, at some point, go back always loomed in the distance. Having made a choice to make the most out of his leave with this return to his hometown of Primrose, he had one month and one mission. To prove to Marnie that he was the one for her and to have her fall helplessly in love with him.

With the anticipation of getting to Primrose, Davis

had his target zoned in on one person and one person only. The object of all his affections, the beautiful Latina he had been dreaming about every night for the past two and a half years, Marnie Perez. From the moment he met her, he knew she was special and someone he needed to have in his life. He had made so many mistakes, so many that he honestly was nervous about seeing her again. Although they had made progress in their relationship through their emails, the anxiety of not knowing how his unexpected return would be received brought every insecurity he had to the forefront. *Would she be happy? Would she be tentative? Would things between them feel awkward and strained?* His head was full of questions and uncertainty about how their reunion would play out. However, when she saw him and their eyes met, his heart leapt from his chest, and he saw the love and longing in her gaze. That unmistakable look you can only give to the person who has captured your heart. Then, when Marnie ran to him and her sweet softness molded against his body in the warmest, most satisfying embrace he had ever experienced, he knew, right there, that he could hold this woman for the rest of his life. That she was his, and he wasn't going to let her get away, ever again. Feeling her emotions spill on his uniform, the wetness of her soft cheeks, the salty taste of her tears, the exquisite feel of her lips, Davis confirmed what his heart already knew. He was hopelessly and irrevocably in love with Marnie Perez.

Now, sitting here at the peninsula in his kitchen, watching her fix each of them a plate of burgers and fries and retrieve them each a soda from the fridge, he couldn't take his eyes off her. He had missed watching her and the grace of her movements that were almost poetic. Then there was her body, a body he had spent night after night lying awake thinking about after their night together. Luscious, ample curves that he could still feel in his hands. Marnie was everything he wanted, and more.

"Here you go," Marnie said affectionately, running her hand over his short brush cut hair as she set down a plate in front of him. Setting her own plate down, she took a seat next to him, and rested her hand on his forearm, her face bright and beaming as she said. "I still can't believe you're here. Does Bea know?"

"Not yet, but I did text Garrett. Bea has one more shift tomorrow and then I thought I would surprise her," he said with a smile. "Garrett and I are in cahoots."

"So, what are you going to do tomorrow, then? It's Sunday and as you know it's tradition to have dinner at my Abuela's house," she said, picking up a french fry. "Do you want to go with me?"

"Am I welcome?" he asked cautiously, his brows knitting together.

Marnie met his gaze with sincerity. "Nobody hates you, Davis. My dad may stare you down, but you're a soldier, so I'm sure you've seen worse." she replied with a wink.

"I have," he chuckled. "Do they know everything?"

"Yes, well, at least the basic details. As you know my family is very involved in each other's lives. We celebrate, we grieve together, and we meddle." She said, rolling her eyes. "Besides, if you don't come with me, Abuela will be heartbroken."

"Well, we can't have that. Will there be tamales?" he asked playfully.

"Of course!" she exclaimed with a smile. "Will you come then?"

Davis leaned in, meeting her expectant gaze. "I would be there with or without the tamales," he replied, then brushed his lips softly to hers as heat rose to her cheeks. He touched her face, feeling the heat under his fingertips and whispered, "So beautiful."

They ate together, sharing stories about his experiences in Africa and her asking so many questions. Marnie's insatiable curiosity had become something he loved about her and although he'd preferred to be in the background watching and listening with Marnie, he found himself caught up in their endless conversation.

After dinner, they washed the dishes together and, realizing it was late, Marnie, always the early riser, let out a huge yawn.

"Am I boring you already?" he asked, feeling his own exhaustion creeping up on him.

"No, sorry." She replied, as another yawn escaped. "I think I need to call it a night, though."

They walked together down the hallway to the bedrooms, both stopping at Davis's bedroom door. Davis glanced at Marnie, trying to read her body language. As much as he wanted to revisit their intense connection in bed, Davis wasn't about to damage the progress of the past months by jumping in too soon. Marnie would have to be the one to take the lead when it came to intimacy. He turned to her, wrapped his hand around her waist, drawing her into him, and reverently brought his lips to hers for a sweet and tender kiss. Pulling away, he cupped her face, staring deep into her dreamy eyes. "Good night, Sugar." Then turned and slipped into his bedroom, shutting the door behind him.

* * *

MARNIE RUSHED into the bathroom and let out a long, swoony sigh. She needed a moment to process her feelings right now. Not expecting him, the sweet surprise of his early return had her mind and heart reeling with a million thoughts and questions. Rekindling their connection these past months via email, getting to know him more and tonight, falling back so effortlessly into conversation, and deep affection for one another was far more than she could have asked for. The difference between before and now, however, was that she was now sure that they were on the same page and the realization of that made her want so much more. Despite their desire for each other, Davis was being a gentleman, and letting her take the lead, which made her love and respect him more.

Marnie prepared herself for bed and slipped out of the bathroom to find Davis waiting, toothbrush and toothpaste in hand, shirtless and pajama pants slung low on his narrow hips. Marnie licked her lips instinctively as she took in his bulky shoulders, muscular chest, and deliciously toned stomach. She loved how thick and burly he was, his body powerful and strong. The memory of him pinning her to the mattress with that hard, heavy body, causing her to grow wet as she looked her fill. Realizing her gaze lingered awkwardly long, a warm flush settled on her cheeks as she smiled and quickly slipped into her bedroom. Closing her door, she leaned against the hard surface, letting out a long breath. Her heart beating rapidly in her chest as she swallowed trying to tamp down her desires. *I can't go there yet, not this soon. We've been through so much we need to take this relationship we're starting, slowly. Sex will just complicate things again, and I won't know if he is truly in love with me if we go too fast.*

Taking in another deep, cleansing breath, she stripped out of her clothes and put on her pajamas. Pulling her shoulder length wavy hair back in a messy ponytail, she climbed into bed and flicked off the lights. In the dark, under her covers, she felt safe thinking about Davis. She lay there a long time, reliving their reunion and conversation tonight, until her eyes became heavy. She closed them, drifting into a dream-like state, and her favorite dream began. Davis before her, his darkening green eyes hungry and full of desire. It was how all her dreams of him started and now, having been in his arms again, she could feel him, how warm and wonderful he felt, his rich musky scent, manly and impossibly sexy. He ran his hands down her body, the feel of his calloused hands, both rough and sweet against her soft skin. She let out a loud drawn-out moan, the erotic sound startling her awake from her half-asleep state. Sitting up suddenly, she surveyed the room. It was just her in the room, but it felt like he was there too, the vision of him so vivid in her mind's eye. A light knock sounded at the door and, as if manifested from her dream, Davis peeked inside, the moonlight from her window casting bands of light over his face.

"Are you okay?" he whispered. "I heard a strange loud sound come from your room and I thought maybe something seriously wrong."

Oh, God, he heard me. Marnie felt the familiar hot flush start at her neck and settle in her cheeks. Grateful the lights were out, and Davis couldn't see her embarrassment, she swallowed down and squeaked out, "No, I'm okay, I just woke from a dream."

Davis entered her room; his brows drawn together with concern. "Did you have a nightmare?"

"No." she replied simply. *I had a sex dream about you,* she internally groaned, feeling slightly mortified.

"Oh, okay, I'm sorry," he started, ready to slip out the door again.

"Wait." Marnie rasped, making Davis double back his eyes, cutting through the faint light from the window. "I want you to sleep with me. I mean, just sleep, no funny business." She said to clarify.

A smile tugged at Davis's lips as he nodded and replied, "I can do that."

Davis came around the free side of the bed and pulled the comforter back, slipping under the covers. Marnie lay back down, and he snuggled in behind her, pressing his hard chest to her back and wrapping his strong arm around her waist. She could feel his breath on her neck, making her shiver.

"Are you cold?" he asked, pulling her closer to his body in a spooning position.

"No, you just feel nice." she sighed, relaxing in his hold, all tension in her body dissipating.

"Goodnight, Sugar." he said, his deep voice soothing as they both drifted off into a contented dreamless sleep.

CHAPTER 11

The light broke through the curtains of Marnie's room, shining bands of light beaming across the bedroom door. Davis's eyes darting around the room as his mind placed where he was. *Marnie's bed.* She wasn't there, so he rolled onto her side and took a deep inhale into her pillow, catching her sweet smell of vanilla and sugar. Davis closed his eyes, wishing he could stay right there, the scent of her enveloping him, but he needed to see the real thing. *Marnie has to be here somewhere.*

Swinging his legs out of bed, he rose and padded out of her bedroom. As soon as he opened the door the smell of butter, brown sugar and cinnamon enveloped him, and his stomach growled, knowing exactly where his woman was. Quickly taking care of his morning needs, he made his way into the kitchen. Rounding the corner into the kitchen, there she was, melting what he assumed was butter on the stove. Still in her sleep tank and shorts and her wavy dark brown hair still pulled up in a messy pony-tail, waves of hair had escaped during sleep, making her look adorably disheveled. An apron on and ear buds in her ears, she shook her hips seductively to the music and although he couldn't hear the song; he was mesmerized by the rhythm and the way her body moved. Leaning against the cased opening, he crossed his arms and legs, watching her. *She is so sexy.* She wiggled in front of the stove, every now and then singing out a note or part of the tune. She was putting on a show and he had the best seat in the house. Grabbing the pot off the stove, Marnie turned and caught sight of him, a slow blush blooming on her cheeks as she set the pot of butter down on a trivet.

"How long have you been watching?" she asked, removing her ear buds, a smile tugging at her lips.

"Long enough." He replied, giving her a mischievous grin as he approached the peninsula, took a seat, and leaned his elbows on the counter, adding, "By all means, continue."

Marnie rolled her eyes at him, and a giggle escaped her throat as he got up from his stool and came around the counter, wrapping his arms around her in a reverse hug and planting a kiss on her neck. "You are so beautiful, Sugar."

Marnie leaned her head back against his shoulder and put her hands over his, resting on her stomach. Davis loved how she responded to him and his touches, the moment feeling very intimate. They stood there a minute enrobed in each other until his stomach growled loudly.

"Hungry?" she asked, glancing over her shoulder to meet his gaze. "I have a batch baked and cooled."

Davis let go of her and returned to his seat facing her. "Please bring it on. Add your incredible cinnamon buns to my list of favorite foods, along with your Abuela's tamales and your Mexican chocolate cake."

"Do you mean this cake?" she said, opening the fridge and showing him a beautifully decorated Mexican chocolate Bundt cake.

Davis let out a groan of approval between bites of his cinnamon bun, then asked, "What time were you up this morning?"

"5 a.m." she replied, shaking her head. "It's hard to break my routine even on my days off."

"I can see that; my internal alarm is always on too." he shared. "But last night, for some reason, I slept more soundly than I have in a long time. Perhaps it was who I was sleeping with," he added with a wink.

"We did get pretty snuggly," she said with a smile as she sprinkled brown sugar and cinnamon mixture over the rolled-out dough. "Sorry, I woke you." She said, wrinkling her nose.

"I'm not sorry," he said, meeting her gaze, eyes dancing, and an amused smile tugging at his lips. "It sounded like a very good dream."

Marnie looked up, meeting his gaze as pink crept up her cheeks. She giggled nervously. "I can't believe you heard that."

Davis popped the last bite into his mouth, joining her in laughter as he rose from his stool, rounded the counter, and put his plate in the sink. Leaning in, his body pressing into her from behind, he whispered, "I hope I hear that sound again soon. That was delicious, Sugar. Thank you." Then he strode out of the kitchen to get ready for the day, knowing she was left wanting him as much as he wanted her.

* * *

DAVIS AND MARNIE pulled into the driveway of her Abuela's house in a newer development of St. Augustine. The two-story home was large and modern, with brown stucco and a cheerful red door. The house looked welcoming, like a place to gather, and that was exactly what it was. The driveway was already full, and it looked like they were one of the last to arrive.

Marnie glanced over to Davis. "You look nervous. Trust me, it will be okay. If my padre pulls you aside for a chat, just nod and tell him we are dating." She informed me. "I think he will feel better if he knows that."

"Are we officially dating, then?" Davis asked, raising his eyebrows at her in question.

"I hope so," she said with a hesitant smile. "At least I want to."

"Then we're dating," he said finally as he reached for her, cupped the back of head, and brought her lips to him for a chaste kiss. "Are you my girlfriend?"

"Yes." she replied, smiling against his lips. "I really want that."

He kissed her again, this time with more passion, sealing their agreement. A knock on the window of the car surprised them both, causing them to break their embrace. The faces of her three youngest brothers greeted them, all smiling with amusement, and Marnie's eyebrows furrowed in frustration.

"Seriously!" she yelled as she opened her door and got out. "Javier, Arturo, Diego, do you understand the concept of privacy?"

"If you're going to make out in a public street, expect an audience." Her youngest 15-year-old brother, Diego, said cheekily.

"Remind me when you have your first girlfriend, to embarrass you thoroughly!" she exclaimed as she rounded the vehicle and gave him a soft slap on the back of the head. The trio of troublemakers retreated across the yard into the house, the echoes of their laughter trailing after them. She shook her head. "Estupido!" she yelled after them.

Marnie turned to Davis, now out of the vehicle, and doubled over with laughter. "Don't encourage them." She said, hand on her hip, gaze pinned on Davis, and an amused smile tugged at her lips.

Davis bridged the gap between them and reached up, cupping her cheek, his eyes dancing with delight as he leaned in and planted a chaste kiss on her lips. Marnie let out a nervous sigh, went back to the side of the car and opened the back door to retrieve the cake she had made. Reaching for his hand, she laced her fingers with his and gave his hand a squeeze as they walked to the front door and, with one last deep breath, stepped inside. The sound of Latin music playing and the echo of loud conversations and laughter echoed through the house.

"Hola Familia! I've brought a guest!" Marnie shouted.

"Mila! My sweet girl is here," a deep voice answered as her father came down the hallway to greet them at the front entrance. He leaned in and kissed Marnie on the cheek, then he let his intense gaze drift to Davis. His mouth pursed tight as his eyes bore into Davis with what could only be described as a death glare.

"Papa, you remember Davis Baxter." she said, gesturing to Davis.

Davis put his hand out to her father and her father squinted, giving him a scrutinizing look as he folded his arms over his chest.

"Papa, be nice." Marnie chided. "Davis and I are dating; he's my boyfriend."

His eyes darted to his daughter, and she nodded in confirmation. When his gaze returned to Davis, his eyes had softened, and a smile tugged at his lips. Unfolding his arms, he took Davis's offered hand, giving it a firm squeeze as if to tell him, "Don't you dare hurt my daughter again" and replied, "Nice to see you again, Davis."

"Nice to see you as well." Davis answered, giving him a genuine smile, seemingly unaffected by her protective father's attempt at intimidation.

While this was happening, the rest of the family had crowded into the entrance, with all eyes on Davis. Like Moses parting the Red Sea, the crowd parted for Abuela, whose arms were already outstretched to him.

"Oh, Davis, you sweetheart! I am so happy to see you. When did you get here?" she asked, bringing him in for a hug and giving him a kiss on the cheek.

"I got in last night. I have a one month leave." He said, taking in all the love she was giving him.

She beamed at him and took his hands in hers. "Then

you must come for family dinner every Sunday while you are here. I insist."

"I would love that," he replied as she took his hand guiding him through the onlooking family into the kitchen where Marnie's Madre stood stirring a pot of beans on the stove.

She turned and, seeing Davis, she set the spoon off to the side and walked up to him, taking his face in her hands. She said nothing at first, just looked him in the eye with her warm rich brown eyes just like Marnie's, then brought his head down, kissing his forehead. The gesture was so affectionate and sweet. That of a mother to a son and Davis felt a lump form in his throat. She returned her gaze to him and said, "We are so happy you are here." Releasing him, she returned to the pot she was stirring and said, "I hope you're hungry because we have a feast here and now it's a celebration!"

With that, the party began. A torrent of food, music, and at one point, dancing filled the house. Davis was bombarded with questions about his mission, about his service, about his plans for the future. To some, their onslaught of questions may have seemed nosy or pointed, but to Davis he liked how straightforward and curious the Perez family was, and he appreciated how they looked out for their own. He understood that kind of loyalty and he loved how to them family was everything.

With a stomach fuller than he could ever remember and heart comparably full, he watched as Marnie talked animatedly with her brother Rami. Her English combined with Spanish doing crazy things to his libido. She caught his stare in her peripheral vision and turned to smile at him, giving him a sly wink. His heart fluttered with her small flirtation and for a moment he couldn't hear the chatter or the music around him. The world stilled, and it was just him and her. *My God, I love her; I love her so much.*

Glancing down at his hands, he stared at them for a moment, lost in thought. *Why have I waited so long to tell her? Why have I held my feelings back? I don't want to lose her again. I can't lose her again. She is it for me.* He looked up at her again, emotion rising to the surface, his pulse quickening. *I need to tell her; I need her to know how I feel.* Perhaps it was the cervezas, the fully satisfied feeling after a truly fantastic meal, or the warm hug of love and protection her family seemed to bring to him, but at that moment, he was drunk. Drunk on his emotions and drunk on his love for Marnie. Davis would never consider himself an audacious man, especially when it came to expressing his emotions, but right now he felt bold. Bolder than he had ever felt in his life, and he needed to profess his love to her. Now this second. He had held back too long, and he knew in his gut she felt the same. With that, he set his drink down, rose to his feet, swallowed away all his doubts and shouted right there in the middle of everyone. "Marnie, I love you!"

The room instantly grew quiet, the music stopped, and all eyes were on Davis. The silence around him was deafening, but Davis held up his chin and repeated his declaration as the words came out in a torrent. "Marnie, I love you. I have since I met you, literally the first day we met," he said, his voice wavering a slight crack coming out with his words. "I love how you are so sweet and kind and how you fiercely love your family and friends. I love how you swear under your breath in Spanish when you think no one is listening and how you dance when you bake. I love how you feel so deeply and passionately about everyone and everything around you. There is not a single thing I don't love about you, Marnie. In my eyes you are perfection," he confessed, the words flowing as Marnie stared at him unblinking from across the room. Taking a deep, steadying breath, a wave of love washed over him, spurring him to continue. "I asked you to marry me months ago, telling you it was the right thing to do, but what I held back was that I wanted to marry you. I wanted to marry you so badly, I couldn't see straight. I wanted you to be my wife, and I wanted us to make a family of our own and be happy together. I still want those things with you, Marnie. That ring you're wearing is still my declaration to you that I want to marry you, and that I will love you till my last breath."

Marnie sucked in a breath, her lashes fluttered, and tears welled up in her beautiful brown eyes. Closing the distance between them, Davis stopped in front of her, put out his hand and she gently lay her hand in his. Slipping the ring off her finger, there in the middle of Abuela's living room Davis dropped to one knee, looked up at the woman he loved more than life itself and asked, "Martina Rosa Catalina Perez, will you do me the honor of becoming my wife. Will you marry me?"

Marnie blinked, tears falling freely down her cheeks she giggled through her tears as she answered in a shout, "YES! I love you too, Davis!"

Davis slipped the ring back on her finger and rose,

sweeping her in his arms as he whispered into her ear, "Now that is how I should have proposed."

Setting her down, Marnie's face happy and radiant, she took his face in her hands and brushed her lips to his. Releasing their kiss, she replied, "That was perfect."

Around them, the Perez family cheered, and they were swarmed with kisses and hugs as celebratory music played. The family celebration, now one of undying love between two souls, as Davis held Marnie tight in his arms.

CHAPTER 12

Shortly after Davis's proposal, they said their goodbyes and headed home to Primrose. As they pulled into the driveway, Marnie looked down at her ring and over to Davis as he parked the car. He rested his head on the headrest and turned to face her, meeting her gaze. "What are you thinking, Sugar?"

Her brows knit together, and she looked down at the ring again. "I was just thinking about when you have to go back."

"I just got here. Please don't think about that yet," he urged, taking her hand and bringing it to his lips. "Let's just enjoy this time together and make the most of it."

Marnie smiled wistfully and nodded. "I know we've been officially engaged for only about two hours now, but I want to marry you soon, if possible, Davis. I don't want you to go back having any doubts whether I'll be right here waiting for you."

Davis sat up straight and asked, "What did you have in mind?"

"In two weeks at Abuela's restaurant," she replied. "Something smallish or as small as you can make it with my family. Just family and our closest friends. Abuela pulled me aside and made me the offer tonight. What do you think?"

He leaned into her, cupped the back of her neck, and brought her lips to his for a deep, sensual kiss. Pulling back ever so slightly, his eyes met hers as he whispered. "Let's do it."

With his answer, all their pent-up passion was unleashed. He kissed her, long and hard, fervidly gliding his tongue against hers in a delicious dance. She let out a sigh of pleasure as she broke their kiss and whispered in his ear. "Take me inside and make love to me."

A coquettish smile carved his lips and heat flashed in his eyes as they eagerly exited the car. He took her hand as they sprinted down the walkway and up the front porch to the front door. Davis scrambled to unlock the door, his hands shaking, and Marnie giggled at his struggle. Calmly, she took the keys, her eyes glued on him as she unlocked the door. Davis let out a long exhale, and a stuttered laugh, amused at how impatient and eager he was to be with her again.

ENTERING THE HOUSE, flashbacks of their first night together started to come back to her and although that night started out hot and frantic with him taking charge of her pleasure, tonight she was going to be the one to take the reins.

Marnie turned to face him, his eyes a burning inferno of desire as her hands came up, running her fingers through his short hair and down the stubble of his strong chin, her finger dipping into the cleft. "Did I ever tell you how much I love this?" she asked, replacing her fingers with her tongue. He groaned, as she blazed a hot trail of kisses over his jaw and down his neck, her tongue tracing the line of collarbone peaking over the collar of his button-down shirt. Her lips leaving his warm skin, she started unbuttoning his shirt slowly, button by button, drawing out a seduction to drive him wild. When his shirt was fully open, she ran her hands over his chest and gripped the sides of his shirt, pulling him closer, as she kissed him hotly and backed down the hallway towards her bedroom. His eyes were dark, lustful, going from such a brilliant green to almost black with feral desire. Remembering how take charge and alpha Davis could be, she could feel him relinquishing control, giving her the driver's seat to drive him wild. Stopping in front of her door, she dropped her hands to the waist of his shorts, teasing the waistband with her fingertips. Davis reached over with his strong muscles and pushed the door open. It banged loudly into the other side of the wall. The intensity building, surging like an electrical current between them, Marnie guided him into the bedroom and towards the bed, then turning him, slipping his open shirt over his shoulders and letting it fall to the floor. She took a moment to admire his strong imposing physique, all hard, sinewy muscle, running her hands over the peaks and plains of his shoulders, arms, chest, back and stomach, the feel of him making her wet and wanton as her needy core pulsed. Reaching for the button of his shorts, she gazed through her long lashes at the man she loved, his breaths labored as he tried to restrain himself and give her the control. Sliding the zipper down, her fingertips just grazing the hardness beneath, he let out a growl, so she reached in, molding her fingers around the ridge of him, making him throw his head back in a long, drawn-out groan.

"Sugar, you're playing dirty," he managed to say as she stroked him over his briefs.

Giving him a seductive smile, she slipped his shorts over his hips, letting them pool at his feet as she pushed him onto the bed. He fell back and braced himself on his elbows as she started unbuttoning her blouse slowly and sensually, giving him a little show. Slipping the blouse off her shoulders, letting it fall to the floor, she undid the button of her shorts and turned, sliding them down her hips and over her round heart-shaped behind. Marnie was aware of Davis's appreciation for her curves, so teasingly she wiggled them down her legs, eliciting another growl from his lips. Glancing over her shoulder, she reached around, undid her bra, and let it slip down her arms to the floor. Marnie could feel his eyes tracking her and the tightly coiled sexual tension in the room building, ready to snap. With one more article of clothing to remove, she bit her lip seductively, hooking her fingers into the sides of her panties as she slowly, sinfully slid them over her behind and down her legs, discarding them with the rest of her clothes. Suddenly his strong hands were on her gripping her hips, pulling her towards him, as he kissed each cheek, and bit one lightly, making her gasp in both shock and desire.

"You have the most perfect ass," he said, kissing where he had bitten then kneading her globes, making her pool at his caresses.

"Davis." she moaned. "I'm supposed to be in charge."

Leaning back again on his elbows, watching with a sexy grin, he replied, "The stage is yours, Sugar."

Marnie moved seductively in front of him, wiggling her hips and eliciting a dark, deep growl from his lips. Slowly she turned, exposing the front of her large, firm breasts, pert and needy. Eyes locked on his, she cupped one breast and played with the pebbled peak as her other hand slowly ran down her stomach, heading south. His eyes flashed with pure lust as he watched her fingers slip between her legs, between her soft folds, to where she pulsed with need, and she moaned. That was all Davis could take. Like a jungle cat, he pounced, swooping her into his arms and laying her out on the bed within a matter of seconds. He covered her body, blazing with heat, and she wrapped her legs around him. Grinding his hardness into the softness of her core, creating tantalizing friction against her pulse point. He brought her breast into his mouth as he sucked in the peak, alternating with delicious licks and gentle bites.

"That feels so good," she moaned as he lavished the other breast with equal attention. His hand roamed south to her apex as he massaged her, making her writhe under his touch. "I want you; I need you inside me," she panted. "Lay back."

He complied as she crouched next to him, leaning

down, brushing her lips to his as her hands roamed low over his abdomen, teasing the waistband of his briefs, then slipped inside to grip the hard length of him. Running her hands down his thick, hard shaft, he groaned with pure satisfaction in his eyes. Shimming his briefs over his strong muscular legs, freeing his manhood, hard and thick. She drank in his magnificent body, remembering how he so thoroughly satisfied her before. Climbing over him, she settled herself over his hips, grinding her core over his thick ridge.

Ridiculously aroused, he groaned, "Protection."

"I'm on birth control now and there's only ever been you, so I'm okay without, if you are," she answered breathlessly.

"I am. There has been no one since you." he panted in reply.

With his answer, she positioned him at her entrance and sank, taking him deep into her body, fully sheathed in her molten heat.

Davis closed his eyes and let out a long, deep groan. Slowly opening his eyes, hooded and dark with desire, he demanded with a growl. "Ride me, Sugar, ride me hard."

Marnie looked down at him, a seductive smile on her face, and shook her head. "Oh, no, we're going to take this nice and slow."

Davis growled in response as she started to move, swiveling her hips with a slow teasing grind. He splayed his hands on her behind, his fingertips digging into the soft flesh as he tried to take control and increase their pace. But Marnie wasn't having it. She was in complete control of both her pleasure and his, and the fact that she was driving him insane with desire was both empowering and heady. Savoring each movement, she made love to him, slowly and sensually reveling in how his body fit hers so perfectly. He caressed her curves, squeezing, kneading, gripping. His caresses were demanding but tender. Feeling the delicious burn of her climax begin to crest, she increased the pace, eliciting a groan of appreciation from him as her need to let go escalated. Leaning forward, she thrust her breasts towards him, and he took her invitation, drawing a nipple deep into his mouth.

"Oh..." she moaned, lost in the sensation of him meeting her thrusts. "I am so close, Davis!" she cried, her voice raspy, almost begging.

He reached between them, massaging her center, his touch causing her to unleash a wild moan as her body gripped him like a vice and he followed, his face lost in exquisite pleasure. She continued to move, grinding and pressing until they came down from the high, love drunk and trembling. Still connected, she dropped her head to his chest, and he stroked her back and over her behind. "That was..." she managed.

"Fucking amazing," he added with a satisfied smile.

"Yes, that." She replied with a giggle as he wrapped his strong arms around her, enveloping her in his embrace.

* * *

THE NEXT MORNING, Marnie went back to work and Davis surprised his sister, Bea, by showing up at her door with a box of Marnie's famous cinnamon buns. Bea was ecstatic and, of course, wanted to be filled in on all the details of his early arrival.

"I still can't believe you're here, Davis!" she exclaimed, wrapping her arms around his waist in yet another hug.

He had missed his sister so much, and seeing her so happy and content with her life truly made him joyful. He and his sister were inseparable growing up and despite their tumultuous relationship with their late mother, they had a great childhood and never felt anything but loved by their grandmother.

"I'll be here for a month," he informed, taking a seat at the kitchen table with Bea taking a seat next to him. "And it will be a jam-packed month, because Marnie and I are getting married in two weeks."

Bea squealed and nearly fell off her chair as a smile curled on her lips. "Well then, you answered my next question. I was wondering how things were between you and Marnie." she laughed, rising from the table and gesturing to the coffee maker. Davis nodded, and she retrieved two coffee cups, pouring them each a mugful. Returning to the table, she set one mug in front of him and inquired, "Give me the scoop. Did you ask her again or just agree the first proposal still stood? I want to know the details."

"I proposed last night in front of all her family at their weekly family dinner." he replied, meeting his sister's curious gaze. "I was just sitting there feeling the love of her family, watching her across the room and thinking I could never love anyone more than her. Then suddenly I needed to tell her how I felt, and I just couldn't wait another moment. So, I stood, gave her a whole monologue on how much I loved her, would always love her and how much I wanted to marry her and spend my life with her. Then before I knew it, I was on one knee, with Nanners ring reproposing."

Bea laughed and clapped her hands excitedly, her eyes dancing with delight. "I would have loved to have seen everyone's faces. I just knew you were a romantic!" she said, giving him a hard punch on the arm. "I knew you loved her."

He feigned a wince as he rubbed where she punched him and replied, "I do love Marnie so much. I know I always have. From the moment we met, I just knew."

"I never thought I'd see the day." Bea said, shaking her head and picking up her coffee mug. "I am so incredibly happy for you, Davis! For both of you!" Bea continued. "Now tell me what you want me to do for the wedding."

CHAPTER 13

*I*n a traditional Mexican family, if you say wedding, everyone pitches in, especially when you have less than two weeks to make it all happen. Leaving the plans to her family, Marnie had only a few things to think of, the dress, the cake, and which friends to add to the guest list.

The cake and guest list were easy, but the dress was a challenge. With Abuela's veil as inspiration, she reached out to Bea for help. Bea had introduced her to Garrett's sister Savanah Smithfield, who was known for her fashion curation and was immediately put to work to find Marnie the perfect dress. Informing them she had found it, Savannah arranged for Bea and Marnie to meet at her townhome in St. Augustine to try it on.

"I'm so nervous." Marnie confessed as they walked up to the front door. "If this doesn't work out, I don't have any other options."

"Savanah is like a fashion fairy. She has worked her magic. Trust me on this. I think you'll love what she's found for you." Bea reassured her as she knocked on Savanah's door.

The door flew open and Savanah, gorgeous as always in all her pink haired fashionista glory, greeted them. "Marnie! Bea! Oh, I'm so excited you're here! I have found you the perfect dress and I can't wait to see you in it!" Savanah exclaimed, her excitement palpable as she invited them inside and lead them up the stairs to the main floor of her townhome. She turned to face them, her face beaming as she added, "When you sent me the photo of your grandmother's veil, I knew exactly who to speak to. I sent them your measurements, and they made it special for you."

"A custom dress?" Marnie asked. "How did you pull that off?"

"I still have a few connections from my modeling days, so I called in a few favors." Savanah shared, waving a hand in the air like it was no big deal. "You deserve a special dress, and I just want you to love it as much as I do. So, come with me. I have it hung up in my spare room." She said, leading her down the hallway. "Try it on and come out to show us."

Marnie closed the door, and a gasp could be heard from behind the door, making Savanah squeal. "It's perfect, simply perfect. I'll be out in a moment." Marnie replied, excitement in her voice.

Bea and Savanah chatted at her kitchen island as they waited until the door to the room opened and Marnie walked out, gliding down the hallway towards them. The stunning white charmeuse featured a crisscross bodice, cap sleeves, and flowed to the ground with a full skirt.

What made the dress unique was the band of bright embroidered flowers around the waist. Intricate gardenias in orange, red and blue.

"Oh my, Marnie, you look incredible!" Bea exclaimed, taking in the dress, then raising her gaze to Marnie's face that was streaked with happy tears. "Oh, sweetie!"

"What do you think?" Savanah asked, tears welling up in her eyes too. "It's perfect, isn't it?"

"I don't know how you did it, but this is exactly what I wanted." Marnie replied through her tears.

Savanah and Bea both wrapped her up in a hug, as Bea exclaimed to Savanah, "Charge me up!"

Marnie looked at her friend and soon to be sister-in-law, her eyes wide. "I can't let you pay for it."

"It's my wedding gift to you," Bea said, taking her hands in hers. "You have made my brother so happy. It's the least I can do."

Another flood of tears escaped; Marnie was overcome by her generosity. A friend who had been there for her through the worst time of her life and now who she wanted to stand with her during the best. "Will you stand beside me as my Maid of Honor?" Marnie asked.

"I would love to." Bea replied, bringing her in for another hug, then turned to Savanah. "Do you think you could find me a dress, too?"

* * *

THE DAY HAD FINALLY ARRIVED, and Davis hadn't seen Marnie since last night. Her mother came and whisked her off, saying it was bad luck to see the bride before the wedding. So Davis was left with a quiet house to get ready on his own.

Davis picked up his formal black UN Peacekeeper uniform dress jacket, slipped it on, and was just buttoning it up when he heard a soft knock on the door. Bea's signature curls entered the room before her and meeting his eyes, she asked. "Almost ready?"

"Yes, I just need to finish putting on my jacket and decorations," he replied.

"Let me help." Bea offered, taking over and doing up the top button then walking over to his dresser, picking up his decorations one by one, pinning each of them on the jacket. Decorations pinned in order, Bea looked up at him, so much sisterly love and pride on her face. "You look so handsome, Davis." He looked down at his adoring sister, who he admired so much. "I'm so incredibly proud of you." she continued going on her tiptoes to give him a kiss on the cheek with tears in her eyes. "Nanners is shining down on you today."

"She would have loved all of this," he added with a nostalgic smile. "She always said there was nothing better than a good wedding."

Bea laughed and nodded in agreement. Her grandmother was always a bit of a hopeless romantic. With one last pat on his chest, Bea looped her arm in his and exclaimed, "Okay, my handsome brother, let's get you hitched!"

THE BLUE CORN was a bustle of excitement. The entire restaurant transformed into a Mexican wedding, rivaling the pages of a wedding magazine. Tables were removed for the ceremony and chairs were lined up, flagging an aisle that ended with a beautiful wall of cascading ropes of colorful flowers. Intricate papel picado in white hung from the ceiling in long lines stretching across the entire space. There were approximately 50 guests attending, and everyone was being guided to their seats by one of the Perez brothers. Davis waited at the front with Hayden Hastings, his best man, next to him, chatting with the minister. Delicious smells were wafting into the ceremony space, promising a feast would follow.

"She's here!" Madre Perez shouted above the chatter and Ramiro took a seat in the corner with his guitar in hand and started to play. Once everyone had taken their seats and quieted down, Davis watched the door, anxiously waiting for the woman who had captured his heart. Rami started to sing a soft acoustic version of "Marry Me" by Train and Bea appeared dressed in a long sapphire blue dress carrying a bright bouquet of gardenia, daisies, and greenery. She smiled lovingly at Garrett as she walked past him and gave her brother a wink as she reached the top of the aisle.

The door to the restaurant opened and Marnie's father entered first, taking the hand of his daughter to help her inside, and Davis's pulse started to race in anticipation of seeing his bride. Marnie's head was bowed as her father straightened out her dress and veil and when she looked up, his jaw slacked at the sight of her. Her dark wavy hair was pinned up, letting tendrils fall to her shoulders framing her beautiful face. Her makeup was natural and soft except for a striking shade of red lipstick that made her full lips look sexy and kissable. An intricate, thin veil was clipped to her hair with gold clips and a single red gardenia was pinned to the side of her hair. His eyes trailed down to her wedding dress that accentuated her curvy figure, embroidery at the waist as unique and vibrant as the bride wearing it. *How did I get so lucky?*

* * *

MARNIE'S BREATH caught as she took in the wedding transformation of her family's restaurant, decked out with color decorations, gorgeous flowers, the entire space a mix of traditional Mexican and modern touches. It was incredible and so much more than she had ever dreamed.

"Do you like it, Mila?" her father whispered, leaning into her.

"I love it, Papa." she replied, looping her arm in his and giving him a grateful smile. "I'm ready to get married."

With a smile, he gave her a nod, and they started down the aisle, to the soft strum of the guitar and Rami's smooth voice as their guests stood. Halfway down the aisle she saw him, her eyes fixed on the man she had spent so many nights dreaming of, who was now waiting for her at the end of the aisle. Dressed in his formal military uniform, Davis looked like something out of a movie and as she walked slowly towards him, it was like no one else was there. Just the two of them. The man she longed to be with, the man she loved so much. Reaching the top of the aisle, his eyes shone, and she smiled wide, feeling emotion well up in her chest and tears fill her eyes at seeing the sheer happiness on his handsome face. He turned to shake her father's hand, and the minister said, "Who gives this woman to this man?"

"Her mother and I do," her father answered, then leaned in to give her a kiss on the cheek as Marnie took Davis's hand.

Davis met her gaze and rasped out, "You are breathtaking."

A slow blush rose to her cheeks with his words, and Marnie beamed up at him, her heart full to bursting with love for this man as she volleyed. "You look pretty fantastic yourself, soldier."

The minister stood in front of them, his folder open as he looked out to the guests, ready to speak. "Welcome everyone! Please be seated." A shuffle of the guests taking their seats filled the room. "We are gathered here together to witness the marriage of Martina Rosa Catalina Perez to Sargeant Davis Aiden Baxter. This is a joyful and wonderful event, so let's lift this couple up in silent prayer as they start the next phase of their journey together." The guests were silent for a moment and the minister continued. "Each couple has a story, a beautiful story which is a combination of their past, present, and future, a story where two people have managed to find each other, both from different places, both down different paths. Yet, their paths meet, and they make the decision to walk together rather than alone. Today we have all shared in their past, are here witnessing their present and will have the joy of seeing their future unfold." Looking from Davis to Marnie, he continued, "So, what words will you take with you on your journey? When I think of marriage, I not only think of the passage from The Bible that most of us are familiar with: "love is patient love is kind". But when I think of a marriage and a couple who have seen their share of storms having come out together hand in hand, I think of the passage that says, "There is no greater love than to lay down one's life for one's friend." Davis looked at Marnie, his gaze one of reverence as the minister continued. "As a soldier Davis knows a thing of two about sacrifice and what it means to lay his life down for someone else, but in this context, it means you commit to love, support, and stand next to each other through all that life brings you. You walk together through every challenge and triumph, and you commit fully to each other for the rest of your lives. May you find great joy and be blessed on your journey. Do you have vows you would like to share?"

Both Davis and Marnie nodded and looked at each other. Marnie gestured for Davis to go first. Davis pulled a notecard from inside his jacket and looked down at Marnie, his eyes gleaming. "Marnie, you know I'm not a man that finds sharing my feelings easy. Seriously, it took me till two weeks ago to finally tell you I loved you," he said with a laugh as he shook his head. "Literally from the day I met you, I knew. From that first day, you completely had me, and I saw no one else, just you. Since then, I feel like I have been building to this day, when I become the luckiest man in the entire world and finally get to call you mine. My wife, my love, forever."

The sounds of amens echoed from the guests and Marnie met his gaze, tears in her eyes as she mouthed, "I love you." Marnie gazed up at Davis, her brown eyes warm and loving. "Davis, when I thought about writing vows to you, I struggled because putting into words how much I love you is difficult for me. I just do. So, I thought I would make you some promises. I promise to encourage you, support you and believe in you. I promise to listen to you with an open heart and an open mind. I promise to be faithful and honest with you, whether we are together or apart. I promise to stand by you and not only be your wife and lover, but your friend. I promise to always make you Mexican Chocolate cake, feed you Abuela's tamales and tell you that I think you are hot every single day." She gave him a wink, and Davis let out a deep laugh. Sniffles and snickers reciprocated from the guests. "And I promise to love you, my husband, my love, forever."

Marnie beamed at him as the minister asked, "Rings?"

Hayden handed the minister two gold bands. "The ring is a symbol of unending love and devotion, a symbol to the world that you are committed to each other, now and always." The minister handed a ring to Davis and as he slid the ring onto Marnie's finger, meeting her gaze with his, he said, "Today, I, Sargeant Davis Aiden Baxter, take you Martina Rosa Catalina Perez to be my wife. I promise to love you through all of life's challenges and triumphs and to be faithful to you all the days of my life. Today and every day I will choose you."

The minister handed Marnie a band, and she slipped it on Davis's finger, then with a shaky voice full of emotion she echoed, "Today, I, Martina Rosa Catalina Perez take you Sargeant Davis Aiden Baxter to be my husband. I promise to love you through all of life's challenges and triumphs and to be faithful to you all the days of my life. Today and every day I will choose you."

Both letting out collective exhales, their faces bursting with anticipation. They looked at the minister. "Then by the power vested in me, I now pronounce you husband and wife. Davis, you may kiss your bride!"

All the guests stood and cheered as Rami started to play a celebration song. Davis took her face in his hands, his eyes sparkling with pure happiness as he lowered his lips to hers in a kiss so tender it made tears fall from her eyes. Releasing their embrace, he kissed her cheeks, capturing the tears, salty and sweet.

"My beautiful wife," he whispered against her cheek. His words were like music to her ears.

* * *

AFTER THE CEREMONY, pictures were taken, and Davis and Marnie stole away into the back office while the family and friends got to work setting up the dinner and celebration.

"Can you help me unclip this veil?" Marnie asked, turning away from Davis.

He gently reached into her hair, releasing the clips holding the veil in place, and once removed, kissed her shoulder sweetly. Together, they folded up the special veil and set it on a shelf. Davis pulled her into him, and she hooked her arms around his neck as she gazed up at him. "Lock the door." She whispered huskily as a coquettish smile curled her red painted lips.

His eyes flashed with desire as he let her go, walked to

the door, and flipped the lock. Turning again to face her, she crooked her finger at him, beckoning him over. He stalked over to her, their mouths crashing in a frantic, wanton kiss. Charged heat between them igniting, his hands made short work of lifting the skirt of her dress as her hands fumbled with the buckle of his black uniform slacks.

"I want you, my sexy soldier husband." She said breathlessly, trying to unbutton his jacket. He took over, pulling it off and laying it gently on a chair, then turned back to her perched on the edge of the desk, her dress pulled all the way up, exposing her white lace thong. He groaned and tugged his pants along with his briefs down his thighs, freeing his hard length. She licked her lips and took him in her hands, stroking as he shifted her panties to the side, finding her wet and ready for him. Positioning himself, he sank into her with one powerful thrust. His wife, on the desk, in her family's restaurant, not caring about anything but how impossibly good it felt to be inside her. She moaned out loudly as he rocked into her, their lovemaking feverish, dirty, and raw.

"Marnie, you feel so good. My beautiful wife."

"Say it again." she begged, meeting his thrusts, her voice breathless with passion.

"My fucking beautiful wife," he growled, making her moan with each thrust of his hips.

"And I fucking love my husband, oh Davis..." she gasped loudly, her body cresting with her release, triggering him to follow.

He let out a deep, guttural groan as his climax ripped through his body and her inner muscles rippled with sweet pleasure around him. Collapsing on top of her, they both let out a quenched sigh. When the last of their tremors subsided and their breathing steadied, Davis helped clean her up and climb off the desk.

Straightening himself up, a loud knock sounded at the door, startling them both, followed by Bea's voice on the other side. "If you two are done getting frisky in there, your guests would like to start dinner."

Marnie's face instantly turned red, and they both burst into laughter as Davis tucked in his shirt, buckled his belt, and reached for his uniform jacket, slipping it back on.

"Well, that was a sweet surprise," he said as Marnie helped him button up his jacket. She looked up at him, her face gorgeously flushed from her orgasm as she deadpanned, "What can I say? There's something about the uniform."

* * *

WHEN THEY EMERGED from the backroom, several servers gave them amused grins and Marnie could feel the hot blush creep up her cheeks. Despite this, she felt no shame about heir little quickie in the office. She had waited a long time to be with Davis, and she was going to enjoy her new husband wherever she could.

Entering the dining room, everyone cheered, whooped, and hollered and Davis made a show of twirling her around, making her giggle. A lovers table was set up for them and guests were already snacking on homemade tortilla chips, salsa and guacamole. Davis pulled out her chair and, as she sat down, she looked around at the transformation. Two long family style tables were set up, one on each side of the room. The tables were dressed with tablecloths and beautiful brightly colored table runners, bouquets of gardenia, roses and daisies, and each table held lanterns for extra light. In the middle was space for dancing, which would commence after dinner.

As Marnie looked out at all the smiling faces, taking in the lively chatter and laughter, she couldn't help but think how blessed she was. Family and friends all gathered to share in their joyous day.

Marnie wiped a stray tear from her cheek and Davis leaned over, his brows knit with concern. "Are you okay, Sugar?"

She giggled and dabbed at her eyes with her cloth napkin. "Yes, it's just everyone is here for us."

"That's because they love us, Marnie. Each person here supports us and loves us," he answered.

He was right. They may be entering into this marriage with questions and unknowns, but they had the support of everyone who loved them and that was more than any new couple could ask for.

CHAPTER 14

The celebration was still going strong when Davis and Marnie changed into casual clothes and bid their farewells to family and friends. Everyone gathered outside the restaurant as Davis pulled up in an Army style jeep as their getaway car.

Marnie's eyes widened at the sight of the big vehicle as she asked, "What's this?"

"My jeep. I bought it years ago, and a military friend has been storing it for me. I got it all fixed up for us as I need a vehicle when I'm on leave. What do you think?"

"I love it!" she exclaimed excitedly as he helped her climb in. She glanced towards the back to find luggage, along with bags of groceries and other supplies. "Where are we headed?"

"You'll find out," he said with a wink.

Honking the horn, Davis and Marnie drove off to start their lives together amid cheers and well wishes from their guests. The sun was kissing the horizon when they drove out of St. Augustine and Marnie gazed out at the beautiful sky with its lingering bright pink, purple, and orange. Everything felt possible tonight, with her love next to her.

Reaching for her hand, Davis threaded his fingers with hers, bringing her hand to his lips to plant a kiss on it. "Happy?" he asked.

"So happy." she replied, looking at her husband dreamily as she rested her head against the seat.

* * *

MARNIE WOKE to Davis's green eyes watching her and his fingers stroking her face. "You fell asleep, Sugar." he said, brushing a tendril of her hair from her eyes. "We're here."

Marnie smiled groggily and sat up, looking around. The shadows of tall evergreens surrounded them, enveloping them in darkness. Off to the side, she could make out what looked like a small cabin and straight ahead a body of water. *A lake maybe.* "What is this place?" she asked, unbuckling her seatbelt and eager to explore.

"This is a fishing cabin both Ben and Hayden own. They bought this property a few years ago as it was a place where they liked to go fishing and build a little cabin here. Ben offered it to me last week and although I'm not really a fisherman, I thought being alone with you in the middle of nowhere sounded like an amazing idea," he said, waggling his eyebrows at her.

"Sounds perfect to me," Marnie said, opening the passenger side door and climbing out. Davis took her hand and led her to the front porch of the small cabin. Feeling around for the key in his pocket, he unlocked the door to the darkened space. Davis felt the wall for a light switch, flicking it on and illuminating the front of the cabin. Marnie walked in, surveying the space. There was a round table off to the side with four chairs, a small kitchen in the corner with a short peninsula, an apartment size fridge, stove, and single sink. Although everything was small scale, it looked new, and the countertops were a beautiful, varnished butcher block. Off to the other side was a chair and a small couch that looked like it pulled out into a bed if needed. "This is nice." Marnie said as she took everything in.

"Let's go check out the bedroom." Davis suggested as they made their way towards the back. Two rooms broke off the main space. A large bedroom and a bathroom. The bathroom was basic, with a large corner shower, a small vanity and toilet. The space was compact, but nice. The bedroom featured a queen-size bed with a beautifully carved headboard that Marnie immediately recognized as Hayden's handiwork. Two end tables flagged the bed, and an armoire sat in the corner. The entire cabin was only around 900 square feet, quaint and cozy. A perfect getaway for two lovers.

Davis pulled her in, wrapping his arms around her, capturing her in a kiss. Their embrace deepened as their voracity for each other coiled and a burning need to have each other heightened. Their lips parting, Davis put his forehead to hers and they stood together, connected, their breaths heavy with need. An intimate moment between two people so deeply in love.

"Let me get everything inside, we'll settle in..." he

suggested, his eyes growing dark with desire. "… and then let me show you how amazing marriage with me will be."

* * *

Davis woke the next morning to the sun streaming through the bedroom window. The reflection of the evergreens outside casting shadows on the wall. The delicious warmth of Marnie curled around him made him feel blissfully content and happy. He sighed and kissed her head, his fingers playing with the waves of her dark hair. His fingertips trailed down her naked back, enjoying the smooth softness of her skin. His beautiful wife, the only woman he wanted to touch, to kiss, to love and take care of, was now all his. He was going to do everything in his power to give her the life she deserved. Starting with deciding on his career. He had at least two more years on this mission and four years left before he could retire from the military. With his Mechanical Engineering degree attained through the military, he knew he could get a good job and support them as well as their future family. He just needed to get through these next years, however difficult they would be to be apart from Marnie.

Marnie stirred, and her eyes fluttered open, meeting his gaze. "Mmm, good morning," she said, pressing her soft naked body to his, hooking her leg more snuggly around his thighs. The feeling of her instantly piquing his body and making him harden. Her hands roamed over his chest and down his taut torso to his manhood. Gripping him, she teased her hands over his length, stroking him.

"Fuck." he groaned out in approval. "That feels so good."

She smiled a naughty smile as she planted hot kisses down his chest, over his abs, and down his happy trail. Rubbing her thumb over the head of his penis, she spread the drop of wetness at the tip and licked her lips. He watched her intently as she lowered her head kissing it first, then opening her mouth to take him in. She had never gone down on him before and the sight of his beautiful wife pleasuring him was one he would dream about when he was away. She toyed and teased him, rounding her tongue until the sensation left him dangling on the edge.

"Sugar, I'm going to come if you don't stop."

She raised an eyebrow at him and took him deeper into her mouth as she moaned around his length. That was all it took. He let go, giving her every ounce of his pleasure as she drank him down and continued to wring him out with her tongue. Letting him go with a pop, she smiled up at him and catching her lust filled gaze, he threw his head back against his pillow with a satisfied groan.

"Good?" she asked, sliding back in next to him.

"So good," he replied, pulling her closer, relishing the feel of their skin against each other.

They lay there for hours, wrapped up in each other, talking, laughing, kissing, and making love. Riding the wave of their passion for each other again and again.

* * *

THEIR SIX DAYS AWAY TOGETHER, isolated from the rest of the world, were blissful. They swam in the lake, tried fishing with the gear in the cabin, they explored the area on hikes and made love every chance they got. Soon the reality of life hit them as they packed up the jeep and headed home. Davis had one more week on his leave, and Marnie planned for her baking assistant and family to keep the bakery open so she could spend every last moment with her husband. They attended a Perez family dinner; they spent time with Bea and her family, and they went for long walks together through town. On one of their walks, they stopped in the park across from the high school and sat on a bench, enjoying the simplicity of just being together. Davis spotted a maple tree and rose from the bench to pluck a leaf, then returned to sit next to Marnie.

"A maple leaf?" she asked.

He nodded, holding it in the palm of his hand. "Did you know a maple leaf is an ancient symbol for love? In China and Japan, they believe the sweet sap that comes from a maple tree represents the sweetness and wonder of love in daily life." He shared, handing her the leaf.

"I didn't know that," she said, taking it and smoothing her fingers over it. "Now every time I see a maple leaf, I'll think about how sweet it is to be married to you. I love you, Davis." she said, planting a tender kiss on his lips and resting her head on his shoulder.

"I love you too, Sugar."

The week went by far too quickly and the weight of Davis leaving loomed over them. Marnie found herself stealing moments alone to cry. She was going to miss him, and the worst part was she wasn't sure when he would return. During their time together they talked about his job in the military and his plans for the future, but there was still so much uncertainty and things to figure out. Despite this Marnie never questioned whether or not Davis would do his best for them and that was all she could ask for.

Davis packed up his duffle bag, and she watched perched on the bed as he slowly dressed in his fatigues, slipped on his combat boots and camouflage jacket. He reached for his blue beret, and she climbed off the bed, putting her hand out for him to give it to her. Turning to face her she set it on his head, the way she remembered him wearing it on the day she met him, and he turned, taking in his reflection in the mirror.

"Did I put it on right?" she asked, meeting his eyes in the mirror.

"Perfect Sugar." he replied with a faint smile.

Marnie could see the sadness in his eyes as he grabbed his duffle bag and hoisted it over his shoulder. He had to leave soon, and Garrett, Amelia and Bea were waiting for him on the front porch. They made their way outside to where everyone stood, solemn and sad. Setting his bag down, Amelia immediately wrapped her arms around his waist with a big hug.

"Oh kiddo, be good for your mom and dad, okay," he said, looking down at her with affection.

"I will." she said, meeting his gaze. "Love you Uncle Davis."

"Love you too, kiddo."

He turned his gaze to Garrett, and the men hugged, clapping each other on the back as brothers do. Bea, with tears in her eyes, wrapped her arms around him and he reciprocated, lifting her off the ground and making her laugh. "I love you, Sis."

"Love you too, Davis."

Then he turned to Marnie, whose face was already wet with tears, and smiled a resigned smile. His eyes glazing over with emotion, a single tear escaped sliding down his cheek and Marnie reached up and caught it. He cupped her face in his large palms and brought her lips to his, holding her there with a kiss. One of longing and acceptance. Longing to stay but accepting that he had a responsibility.

"I need to go," he whispered against her lips, ending their farewell too soon. He pulled her in, holding her tightly, enrobing her in the warmth of his body as she inhaled his masculine scent, trying to commit it to memory. Desperately wishing he didn't have to go, he kissed her head, released her, and reached for his duffle bag.

"Goodbye." she whispered, wiping the tears from her face. "I love you."

"I love you too, Sugar." he reciprocated with a melancholy smile as he turned and descended the stairs.

Marnie watched as he threw his bag into the trunk and opened the driver's side door of his rental car. She held onto the post of the porch, needing it to keep herself upright, before she crumpled into a sorrowful mess. As she watched the love of her life get into the vehicle, she felt like she was outside her body as she yelled across the lawn, "Davis, wait!"

As if her feet moved on their own, she bounded down the porch steps and ran to him as he stood by the car, almost knocking him over and crashing her lips into his. He let out a grunt, followed by a small chuckle, then kissed her back, passionately, wanting, needing one last kiss from her loving husband. She peeled herself from his body, slowly backed away, and said, "Come back to me."

He gave her a nod and replied, "I will, Sugar, I promise."

CHAPTER 15

In the months that passed, Marnie poured all her time and energy into her business. It had been good before, but with word of mouth from locals and neighboring communities, business was booming. Inundated with custom orders, Marnie hired more help for the front of the bakery and to do the usual daily baking so she could keep up with the demand. With two baking assistants, and three new employees working evenings and weekends, she found herself with more free time, therefore more time to think about Davis.

Six months had passed since Davis returned to his mission, and they emailed each other several times a week, trying to video chat whenever possible. Seeing his face and knowing he was safe was all she needed to move forward through the days ahead. Knowing that his job as a peacekeeper was so much safer than other military jobs, she still couldn't help but worry about him. His expertise was needed on special missions and because of that they sometimes would go weeks without contact when he was called away. Those days would tick by excruciatingly slow and many times she found herself over at Bea and Garrett's house crying into her coffee. Being a military wife was not for the faint of heart.

Email from Marnie Perez @ Everything you Knead to Sergeant Davis Baxter, Canadian Armed Forces – UN Peacekeepers:

Hello, my hot and sexy husband,

I got your email that you're back safe at base camp and will be there for a while. Every time they send you away, I feel like I can't let out a full breath, like I'm holding my breath, waiting for your email telling me that you're safe. I know you probably hate to hear that, but it's true. I pray every day that you're okay and that things don't escalate there. I find myself researching your mission and reading all the information I can get about what you're doing. The work you do is important and know that every day I'm proud of you. You've sacrificed so much, so know that even when I say I miss you, and the pain of not having you here feels like too much, know I'm proud of who you are and that I'm lucky enough to be with you for the rest of my life.

Waiting for you always,

Your Sugar, Marnie

Email from Sergeant Davis Baxter, Canadian Armed Forces Canada – UN Peacekeepers to Marnie Perez @ Everything you Knead:

Hello, my hot as hell Wife,

I assure you, Sugar, I'm the lucky one. I can only imagine how hard it is for you to not be able to contact me. Know that it's

difficult for me too. Although my days are busy, I always think of you and dream about you at night. Sometimes when I close my eyes, I can feel you, your warm soft body under me. How we fit together, and move together, I wake up wishing the dream were real. Trust me, I will be doing dirty things to you when I see you next. My imagination has been running wild. Be prepared to be very satisfied, Sugar.
Lonely without you,
Your Davis

Email from Marnie Perez @ Everything you Knead to Sargeant Davis Baxter, Canadian Armed Forces – UN Peacekeepers:
Hello, my sexy, horny Husband:
Well, now I'm intrigued. Trust me, I have a few ideas for you as well. But until then, I just have our wedding photos, which turned out amazing (see attached) and the memory of our post marital quickie in the restaurant office. Some of the serving staff still won't look me in the eye! That was an incredible day, though. I still can't believe how my family managed to pull that whole thing together so quickly. Pick out the pictures you like, and I will get them framed. I want to fill our house with pictures and memories. I hope you don't mind me taking on a few of the house projects. I've painted the living room and want to paint the bedroom. I was considering doing some kitchen renovations, but I happen to love our little retro kitchen, so I decided to keep it as is. It may seem silly, but I think it is cute, and it inspires me to create. I have to say, I'm grateful for the projects as they help me stay busy. Question, do you want me to clean out your room? I think as my room is the master bedroom, you would want to have everything moved into there.

*And who knows, we may need that room someday. Let me
know.*
Miss, you like crazy
Your loving Wife Marnie

Email from Sergeant Davis Baxter, Canadian Armed
Forces – UN Peacekeepers to Marnie Perez @ Everything
you Knead:
Hello my beautiful Wife,
*It's been 9 months since we married, and I think of that day,
every day. I look at our wedding photos and remember how
amazing the day was, but what I think about the most is how
beautiful you looked in that dress. You always look beautiful,
but that day you glowed, and I want to see that happiness in
your face again. Today I got some bad news, my request for
leave in June for our anniversary was turned down. Too many
important projects I'm working on here that need completing.
I'll be able to reapply in 3 months and will try to get home to
you soon. I hate that you'll be alone for our first anniversary.
But I will try to do something special for you. Stay strong,
Sugar and know I am doing my best.*
Loving and missing you,
Davis

Marnie tried to focus on the cake in front of her, but
all she could think about was Davis. Tomorrow would be
their one-year anniversary, and she hadn't heard from
him in five days. She missed him terribly, but she knew he
had done everything he could to come home to her. She
was starting to understand the system and the nuances of
being a military wife. One thing that helped was a local

support group she found. They would meet once a month, discuss challenges, and encourage each other. She was part of an online group as well, which really helped give her better insight into what to expect and when. Mostly these groups helped her to not feel so alone, and she was now feeling resigned to all those things that she had no control over. Then there were her friends, particularly Bea, who had become her rock and sounding board through the challenges.

Bea popped her head into the back kitchen, her flash of red hair a welcome distraction. "Hey there Sis!"

Marnie liked the fact that she was referring to her as her sister. She had always wanted a sister and Bea in her books was a great one to have. "Hey! What brings you in today?"

"Just wanted to check up on you," she said, striding over to the counter and taking a seat. "Tomorrow's your anniversary. How are you doing?"

"I'm okay. Managing, I guess," Marnie replied, giving Bea a resigned smile. "It sucks that Davis couldn't get leave, but not much we can do."

"I know, it's hard. Just hang in there. My brother loves you so much." Bea said, offering her a compassionate smile.

"I don't doubt that, even for a second." Marnie replied, her brows knit together. "It's just him not able to be here and the fact that it's been a few days since I've gotten an email…" she hesitated. "I guess I'm getting in my head a bit."

"I get that. Waiting isn't easy." she commiserated. "So, I was thinking I could provide you with a little distraction.

Perhaps you could come over tomorrow night for dinner and we can celebrate."

Marnie smiled, thinking how much better that plan sounded than sitting at home, crying in front of her laptop, and staring at her inbox for an email from Davis. "I like that idea."

THE NEXT DAY Marnie still had no email from Davis, and her anxiety was at an all-time high. She was never more grateful for the distraction of dinner with Garrett, Bea, and Amelia.

"Auntie Marnie!" Amelia greeted, giving her an enormous hug. Amelia, now nine years old, was tall for her age and sported a full set of teeth, her adorable lisp now just a fond memory. Marnie had spent a lot of time with her over the years and enjoyed her sweet yet sassy attitude.

"Hey there, kiddo! How's my favorite niece?"

Amelia put her hand on her hip and cocked her head to the side at Marnie. "I'm your only niece!"

Marnie laughed at her sass, and replied, "Oh yeah, that's right! But you're still my favorite!" Amelia gave her another big hug and looked at what Marnie had in her hand, her eyes widening. "Can you give this to your mom, but be careful." she said, handing the little girl a freshly made lemon meringue pie. The little girl licked her lips as she carefully walked towards the kitchen with it in both of her hands.

"In here!" Bea exclaimed as Marnie rounded into their

large kitchen. The savory smell of spiced lamb, carrots, celery, and onions wafting towards her was heavenly.

"Are you making what I think you're making?" Marnie asked, coming around the island and peeking into the cast iron pan on the stove.

"If you're thinking of Nanners Shepherd's pie, then yes!" Bea exclaimed with a smile. "Want a glass of wine?"

"Please." Marnie replied, taking a seat at the kitchen island. Bea poured her a glass of red wine and Garrett came inside from the back patio to greet her. "Have you heard from Davis this week?" she asked them both.

Both shook their heads as Bea replied, "I haven't. But don't read too much into it. It can happen where he's unable to communicate for a few days. He hasn't forgotten about your anniversary, though." Bea said with a smile as she reached for a little gift bag on the side of the island, then handed it to her. "And these," she said, slipping into the kitchen pantry and coming out with a large vase filled with gardenias, daisies, and roses, very similar to the flowers at their wedding a year ago.

Marnie took the vase, and a wide smile brightened her face. Her husband had proven himself to always be so thoughtful and even when they weren't able to be together, he always found a way of reminding her that he loved her and was thinking of her. Marnie's phone buzzed, and she pulled it out of her pocket. Sliding it open, she saw an email notification. It was Davis. Marnie felt her heart jump at seeing his name. Bea cocked an eyebrow at her in question. "It's him!" Marnie exclaimed. Opening her emails, she read:

Email from Sargeant Davis Baxter, Canadian Armed Forces – UN Peacekeepers to Marnie Perez @ Everything you Knead:

Happy Anniversary Sugar! I hope you're close to a laptop because I'm going to try to video chat. Here is the link.

"Bea, can I borrow your laptop? Davis can video chat right now," Marnie shared excitedly.

Bea sprang into action and had her laptop set up on the kitchen table in short order. Marnie felt her heart beat wildly in her chest as she waited for the video chat to start up and she clicked the link he gave her. The screen glitched a few times as he came into focus. She felt all the air whoosh from her lungs as she stared into the beautiful green eyes of her loving husband.

"Sugar." he said with emotion in his voice. "I'm so sorry it's been so long since you've heard from me. We had some complications here with the communication system and it's taken a while to get it fixed. I've missed you so much." Tears filled Marnie's eyes, as all the worry of the past week and the emotion of seeing him now on the screen hit her all at once. "Don't cry, Sugar. I'm okay," he said, his brows furrowed.

"I just love you and miss you so much." she rasped, tears rolling down her face.

"I know, I love you. Happy Anniversary. I wish I could be there with you. Hold you, kiss you, do other things to you," he said, his voice going growly as he waggled his eyebrows at her.

She let out a laugh between her tears and looked towards Bea and Garrett, who were leaning on the island, obviously listening. Both rounded the island and came around to join Marnie on the screen, Bea giving Davis a little wave.

"Hey there, little brother! I'm so glad to see you're okay." Bea exclaimed.

"Hey there Davis!" Garrett added. "We're going out to the patio so we can give you two some time alone."

"Love you, Davis!"

"Love you too, Sis." he replied, raising his hand in a wave.

Bea and Garrett slipped out the back door and Marnie brought her eyes back to her husband on the screen. "You look so good," she said, wiping the wetness from her cheeks and smiling.

"You look gorgeous. I miss you so much it's painful some days." he confessed. "I've reapplied for leave and they think I should be able to get time off in the Fall. I know that's a long way away, but honestly, I will take whatever I can get. I just need to be with you."

"I need that too, Davis, so very much." Marnie replied.

"Did Bea give you the flowers and my gift?" he asked with a smile.

Marnie's eyes gleamed as she looked towards the counter and replied, "She did! Just one moment." She got up and retrieved his gifts from the counter, then sat down again, showing him. "The flowers are gorgeous, but I haven't opened the gift yet."

"Go ahead then." He gestured, and she flashed him a smile as she reached into the bag, pulling out the tissue, one by one, making him chuckle. Reaching to the bottom of the bag, she pulled out a long flat velvet box and her eyes darted to meet him.

"What's this?" she asked curiously as she opened the box and her eyes widened with surprise. There in the box was a simple gold chain with a Maple Leaf pendant and a dangling diamond shimmering in the middle. "It's beautiful!" she exclaimed, turning it to show him.

"I wanted to give you something that reminded you of our time together and to let you know that being your husband this past year has been so sweet.", he said with a wink. Marnie grinned and met his gaze on the screen, remembering their conversation about maple leaves almost a year ago. "Do you like it?" he asked. "I know it's not much, but I hope it makes you think of us."

"Two prairie hearts." She mused, looking down at his meaningful gift.

"Exactly." he replied with a smile. "I'm so sorry, but I have to go because others are waiting, but I want you to know that being your husband is the best gift I could ever have. You make me so happy, Marnie."

"You make me happy too, Davis."

"Talk to you later Sugar, I love you too. I will email and keep you posted on my leave request."

"I love you too, Davis." she replied, and blew him a kiss as the screen went static.

Marnie looked down at the beautiful gift from Davis and smiled. Taking the necklace out, she reached behind her head to fasten it around her neck. Lifting the pendant, the diamond in the middle glinted like a wink from her husband. She held the pendant tight in her hand, closed her eyes and sighed, feeling content and ready to take on the months ahead.

CHAPTER 16

Summer flew by and the colder weather of fall started to settle in. Primrose was a wash of rich browns, reds, oranges, and yellows. The leaves were turning, and the promise of colder weather was on the horizon. Marnie found herself going for long walks around town and everywhere she went, she found maple leaves in her path. She would find herself picking them up and taking in their intricacies. The patterned lines within and pointed peaks. Of course, she always thought of Davis and would touch her pendant around her neck, closing her eyes a moment to see his handsome face. They had been through so much, and being away from each other for such long periods of time was difficult. It could test the best of relationships, but in their case, it seemed to make them love each other more. They were two prairie hearts that needed to beat together to make this work. So, if Davis could sacrifice, so could she by waiting for him.

At the end of September, Marnie got word from Davis that he was granted leave and would be home at the end of October. She would have two weeks with her husband, and she couldn't wait. Planning for her staff and family to take over the bakery during his leave, she was determined not to waste a single moment that they had together.

Opting to meet him at the airport, Marnie drove his jeep to Winnipeg, feeling excited and nervous about seeing her husband. It had been 16 months since she had been with him and felt his arms around her and she was more than ready for their reunion. Checking the arrivals board, she smiled, seeing his flight had just arrived. Anxiously, Marnie waited with other families and friends as the doors opened and passengers descended the escalator. As she watched the passengers be greeted by their loved ones, her eyes darted around, emotion rising in her chest with anticipation. The first thing she spotted was the blue beret and then his signature red hair. His eyes drifted over the crowd, then he spotted her, and a slow smile curved his lips as he descended the escalator. As Davis stepped off the escalator, Marnie, with tears welling up in her eyes, navigated her way through the onslaught of passengers wanting nothing more than to feel his strong arms around her. Finally reaching him, Davis dropped his duffle bag to the ground. As she jumped into his arms, their lips crashing together, all the emotion, the longing, the desire culminating in one long-awaited kiss.

Breaking their kiss, foreheads connected, Davis sucked in a breath as he declared. "I missed you so much, Sugar. I love you."

Marnie clung to him, gripping his uniform jacket tight, not wanting to let him go. "I missed you too. Oh, God, Davis, I love you so much."

Many of the crowd that had gathered to welcome home loved ones turned, watching them, smiles on their faces and tears in their eyes as they became spectators of their reunion. One person passed them and patted Davis on his back, saying, "Thank you for your service, man." and some onlookers clapped and cheered. Yet in that sweet moment, as they embraced and shed tears of happiness in each other's arms, it felt like it was only the two of them.

* * *

THE DRIVE HOME was excruciatingly long. Davis insisted on driving, and Marnie spent the entire time leaning into him, her hand laced with his. He lifted their hands and kissed the back of her hand affectionately, Marnie gazing at him, her melting chocolate brown eyes twinkling with pure happiness and, deep in their depths, desire. She ran her hand over his head, her fingertips massaging the back of his scalp, making his pulse spike from her affectionate touch. Davis shifted in his seat, his arousal fully at attention as Marnie trailed her fingers down his neck to the ridge of his collarbone. *Her hands aren't even heading south and she's driving me wild.* The sweet smell of her strawberry shampoo swirled in the cab of the jeep and Davis sucked in a breath, doing everything he could to stay on the road and not get distracted by the goddess next to him. Marnie stared at him through her long lashes with a coquettish grin on her face.

"Don't look at me like that, or I'm going to have to pull

over and do dirty things to you right here in this jeep," he said, his voice husky with need.

"What's stopping you?" she replied, running her hand over his thigh and giving it a firm squeeze.

"Marnie." he growled low and deep as she slowly reached for the hem of the skirt she was wearing and rolled it up to expose her creamy thighs. Another growl escaped his throat as he looked around, spotting a utility road just ahead. Turning sharply onto the road, the sun had almost set and so if they parked on the road, they shouldn't attract the attention of local traffic. Gravel kicking up around them, once they were far enough down the road, Davis put the jeep into park, and turned to Marnie, who was unfastening her seat belt. She reached up under her skirt and shimmied, sliding her panties down her legs. Eagerly, he unbuckled his seat belt and climbed over the console to the backseat. "More room back here," he said as he removed his jacket and frantically started unbuckling his belt. Climbing into the back seat, Marnie slid down his fatigue pants and his boxer briefs, letting his hard length spring free. Her hand gripped him, causing a zing of sensation to shoot up his spine. *I need her. I need her now.*

"Get on my lap," Davis ordered, his breaths coming out labored as she stroked him. Marnie maneuvered onto his lap and straddled his hips, then slid off her jacket and started unbuttoning her blouse. Before she could finish, he dipped his lips to her breasts, kissing the swells. She positioned him at her entrance and with one slide, he was fully sheathed in the warmth of her body, and they both let out a satisfied sigh.

"Fuck me," he growled, as he pulled down a cup of her bra and brought the pebbled peak into his mouth as she ground her hips into him. Her body was so deliciously warm and tight. Stars started to form behind his eyes.

"You feel so good, Davis. I've missed this," she cried, as she rocked her body over him, creating a delicious friction. Throwing her head back, his hands under her skirt, he caressed her behind, relishing their connection and her body all for him. They moved together, feverish and frenzied, the inside of the jeep becoming hot and steamy, causing the windows to fog up and sweat to form on their half-dressed bodies. With husky moans she ground on him harder, using his broad shoulders to leverage herself, her rise and fall increasing, as she chased her orgasm as well as his. Her body gripped him, a telltale sign that his beautiful wife was on the brink.

"Come for me, Sugar. Take what you need." With his words, her body tightened, and she unleashed a long-drawn-out moan, the sounds from her lips so raw and fevered he followed in quick succession, releasing all his pent-up desire into his wife. Collapsing on him, her face burying in his shoulder, he wrapped his arms around her sweat slick body as they shivered and caught their breaths.

Marnie lifted her head and took his face in her hands, planting a passionate kiss on his lips, their tongues tangling together in a sweet dance. Releasing their kiss, she slid off his lap and started buttoning her blouse. He swooped her onto him again, making her giggle.

"Sugar, you better be ready to be naked for the next two weeks." he said as he leaned in and nipped at her cleavage. "Because you and I have a lot of time to make up."

FOR THE FIRST week they did just that, only rolling out of bed for absolute necessities. They explored every facet of their intimacy until both could no longer deny the world outside their tawdry love bubble. Bea was eager to see Davis and the Dia de los Muertos, or Day of the Dead holiday, was about to begin, so they promised Marnie's family they would partake in a special family dinner at the Blue Corn. When they entered the restaurant the familiar sound of loud voices, laughter, and music playing greeted them. Abuela, spotting them from across the room, was the first to greet them.

"Hello Abuela! Coma estas?" Davis said, taking her offered hands and leaning down to let her kiss his cheek.

Impressed, Marnie nodded and gave him a look of approval at his Spanish.

"Oh Mi Carino, Davis!" she said affectionately, hands on his cheeks. "We have missed your handsome face."

Davis and Marnie laughed as everyone came up shaking hands and patting their backs. Rami was the only one missing, as his band was currently on tour.

The entire restaurant had its usual colorful and vibrant décor. The tables, however, were different, long family style tables similar to the ones at their wedding were draped with long tablecloths and decorated with roses, marigolds, and lit candles. Paper fans adorned each place setting and intricately painted skulls sat amongst the candles on the table. Off in one corner was a Day of the Dead altar, or ofrenda, set up with framed pictures, lit candles, flowers, and stacks of fruit. Marnie guided Davis towards the altar as they took in the pictures of deceased family members. Marnie explained who each person was, and she kissed her hand, touching the picture of her late Abuelo. Marnie had brought some flowers and laid them next to a frame that had no picture but had the initials "DJ" within the frame.

"Who is this for?" Davis asked curiously.

Marnie gazed up at him, her big, expressive eyes brimming with tears. "Our baby," she whispered almost inaudibly as she rested her head on his shoulder and squeezed his hand. "I never knew if our baby was a boy or girl, but I felt in my heart it was a boy. I named him Davis Jr."

"You did?" he asked, his eyes full of emotion. "You never told me."

"I'm sorry, it was just too hard to talk about."

Davis put his arm around her supportively and pulled her closer as they stared down at the name of the child they lost.

DAVIS HAD BEEN QUIETER than usual the rest of the night. Although he visited with family and took part in their traditional celebration, he had a solemnness in his demeanor that wasn't like him. Marnie crawled into bed, curling herself around his body, his strong arm pulling her in tight. Not a word passing between them. They lay there a long time in silence, yet Marnie could almost hear Davis's racing thoughts. "Are you okay?"

He opened his mouth to reply, then shut it as if thinking about what to say and how to say it. She looked up at him, her brown eyes imploring him to open to her. "Tonight, there was just a lot to take in," he confessed, meeting her with a melancholy gaze. "Seeing the altar tonight made me think of those that I've lost, and it made me think of our baby. Seeing that was just a reminder of what could have been."

"I'm sorry again, if you weren't expecting it and I'm sorry I never shared with you what I named him." She said, reaching up to tenderly caress his cheek.

He looked down at her affectionately and smoothed a hand over her hair. "I understand why you didn't," he reassured her. "I'm not upset with you." Marnie let out a sigh of relief and settled her head back onto his chest. "Thank you for naming him after me."

Marnie smiled wistfully and snuggled into him tighter. "I think of him sometimes and wonder what it would be like if he were with us right now. We would be parents to a toddler."

Davis kissed her head, then asked, "Do you want to try again? Are you able to try again? This time planned, of course."

"I do want to and yes, I'm able. The doctor reassured me that DJ's stillbirth was nothing I did or anything my body did. It just wasn't meant to be," she replied. "Why are you asking?"

"I don't know. I've been just thinking about it a lot lately." He replied. "It would be nice to have a little one, a little like me, a little like you. I mean, the timing may be off and the chances may be slim right now, but we can plan to try for a family the next time I'm back. I only have two and a half years left before I can request retirement and be home permanently."

"Then we wait." Marnie replied simply, meeting his gaze.

"Are you sure?" he asked, searching her eyes.

"I want you to experience everything with me, and I don't want to do it all alone. I'm still young." She replied. "We have time."

He nodded and kissed her head affectionately. "Until then, can we practice and make sure we have this baby making thing down?" he asked, with a waggle of his eyebrows.

"Yes sir!" She exclaimed with a salute.

"How about I salute you?" he replied, rolling over and covering her with his hard, heavy body as his hips pinned her to the mattress.

"I think we are going to need lots and lots of practice." she answered with a coquettish smile as she brought him in for a passionate kiss and she whispered against his mouth, "Show me what you got, soldier."

* * *

THEIR TWO WEEKS together ended far too quickly, and as she saw Davis off yet again, this time, she felt stronger and more prepared for the year ahead. In their brief time together, they had made decisions for their future, and she came away from his visit feeling excited about what was in store for them.

The year went by with dozens of emails, video calls when able, and another anniversary passed with them still apart. As summer turned to fall, Marnie leaned on her family and friends more and more. Bea, Ever and Whitney were there every week like clockwork, giving her a much-needed distraction and encouragement.

Their families were growing with Ever having added a baby boy to their gaggle of girls. Whitney had become the ultimate boy mom with three boys under the age of four and Bea was still trying to add to her family but continuing to be optimistic. Sometimes she felt jealous, like her life was on hold while theirs was full steam ahead. Despite this, she was committed to Davis and would wait till the timing was right and he was home for good.

"Hello ladies! How's everyone doing today?" Marnie greeted coming around and taking a seat with her friends. "Give me that baby, Ever."

Ever laughed and handed Luke over to her. He smiled when she took him, and she kissed his chubby cheeks. Bea looked at Marnie, who cooed at Luke, making him giggle.

"You look good holding him. Any thoughts about starting a family?" Bea asked, taking a sip of her coffee.

"Yes, and no," she replied, smiling at her friends. "Yes, we want to start a family. No, not yet. Not until Davis puts in his request to retire, so approximately two more years."

"I understand that. I can't imagine not having Hayden around to help with the boys." Whitney commented.

"I agree." Ever added. "Also, the possibility of not

having Ben there during the birth would be difficult to get my head around."

Marnie brought Luke to her chest, cuddling him. "I mean, lots of military wives do it and manage just fine, but I really want him home. We're so close to his retirement that I just need to be patient."

"I think that's a good plan. I know with us never knowing our father, Davis wants to be present for his kids. He's going to be an amazing father." Bea reflected.

Marnie smiled and leaned into Luke to smell his sweet baby powder scent, knowing someday she would be holding a baby of their own.

CHAPTER 17

Fall turned cold and a light dusting of snow blanketed the town, making it sparkle like a winter wonderland just in time for the holiday season. When not inundated with orders at the bakery, Marnie participated in the holiday community events around town, getting lost in the festivities alongside local friends and neighbors. Every day she was grateful for the love and support of those around her, helping her get through the lonely times without Davis.

Marnie's alarm buzzed, and she rolled out of bed – 4 a.m. 5 days till Christmas and she needed to rush to get ready so she could get off to an early start. Today was one of those days she wished she could stay in bed just a little bit longer. A cold snap had come through their area and the frigid chill outside wasn't nearly as appealing as the warm cocoon of her bed. She reached for her phone and opened it. A smile curled her lips as she saw an email from Davis. Clicking on it, the email read:

Email from Sergeant Davis Baxter, Canadian Armed Forces – UN Peacekeepers to Marnie Perez @ Everything you Knead:

My sweet Marnie,

I found out today that I'm being sent out on a special mission for at least the next week, so I'll likely be unable to contact you until after Christmas. They need my help with a construction site in a remote location to repair some equipment, and we're not sure how long it will take. I might be back in time for Christmas, but it's hard to tell, so I can't promise you I will be. I do promise you that you'll be in my thoughts every hour of every day. I love you, Sugar. More than life itself. I'll come back to you. I promise.

All my love, Davis

Marnie held her phone to chest and sighed. Hearing his declaration of love was something that would fuel her through her day. She put her phone down on her bed and rummaged through drawers and her closet, setting out her clothes for the day. Slipping out of her room, she made her way to the bathroom to shower and get ready. When she returned, she slipped on her clothes and reached for her phone to put it in her pocket. It buzzed, and she opened it curiously. Two missed calls, a voice mail. That was strange. Who would be calling her this early in the morning? No one was usually up at this hour but her. She pressed her voice mail button and as she did, her phone rang, an incoming call. Bea's name popped up on the screen and Marnie's brows furrowed with concern as she quickly answered it. Before she could greet her, Bea interrupted, her voice frantic and shaky.

"Marnie, Davis has been in an accident." Shock slapped her in the face as Marnie sat on the edge of the bed, Bea's words slowly repeating in her head. *Davis has been in an accident.* "I just got a call, Marnie. They tried to call you but couldn't reach you. I'm his next of kin after you," she explained. "I'm coming over."

Minutes later, Marnie heard the familiar click of the door opening and Bea's footsteps hurriedly coming down the hall. She opened her bedroom door and Marnie looked up at Bea, meeting her wide with worried eyes. Marnie stood with her phone held limply in her hand. "I need to go to work," she said, shaking her head, denial in her tone as she rose from the bed.

"Marnie, sweetie, did you hear me on the phone?" Bea asked, emotion thick in her voice, trying to meet her gaze. "Davis has been in an accident."

The words absorbed into her brain as the initial shock subsided. "What?" she asked, as if she had not heard her correctly.

"Davis has been in an accident, sweetie. On a construction site. He is critical but stable. They are airlifting him to a medical facility in Germany."

The sharp sting of tears pricked her eyes, and her chest tightened painfully. "Is he going to be okay?" she whispered, her chin now quivering.

"I don't know Marnie. I honestly don't know." Bea replied, her voice cracking as tears welled up in her eyes and she wrapped her arms around her. "They said they're going to call again when they know more. All we can do while we wait is pray."

Marnie sank to the bed again and Bea curled herself

around her as she tried to reassure her. "Davis is a fighter. He's so strong. I know he'll be okay. He has to be okay."

* * *

THE MORNING DRAGGED ON, with no further word on Davis's injuries or condition. Bea called in Marnie's family to take over the bakery and her Abuela and Madre came over busying themselves in the kitchen fixing food for everyone that had gathered in support. Friends and family came and went, Ever and Whitney rushed over and sat with Marnie as they waited. The afternoon drew near, still with no word, and soon the shadows of the early evening started to descend.

"Mila, you need to eat," her Madre urged, putting a plate of food in front of her. "You need your strength."

Marnie pushed the plate away as more tears threatened to spill and she wrapped herself tighter in her comforter, allowing it to protect her from what she was sure was the inevitable. Her mind had explored every possibility as they waited, but each time settled on that Davis was never coming back to her. They had no answers and as the minutes ticked by with nothing, all hope seemed to fade. By the time the clock struck 7 p.m. everyone was quiet, heads hung low, all optimism gone. Then Marnie's phone rang from the coffee table, awakening the sorrowful scene and everyone looked up, glimmers of hope in their eyes.

Bea grabbed the phone and answered. "Hello? No, this is Davis's sister, but his wife is right here. Let me put you on speaker phone." Bea pressed a button and held up the phone. Everyone in the house gathering in the living room.

"Mrs. Baxter, your husband was critically injured on a remote construction site. A piece of machinery rolled onto him, crushing his left leg. He lost a lot of blood, but we were able to stabilize him and transport him to a military hospital in Germany. He's currently in surgery. Ma'am, they're doing everything they can to try to save his leg."

Marnie's breath caught at his words, and she covered her mouth.

Bea continued. "Is he going to be okay?"

"It's hard to say at this moment, Ma'am, as they are still uncovering the extent of his injuries and we will call again after he's out of surgery, and we have more information."

"Thank you, sir." Bea hung up the phone and a collective exhale sounded in the room; everyone having held their breaths during the call. Bea sat down next to Marnie and took her hand in hers. "He's alive, Marnie. He's alive, and that is all that matters."

* * *

THE NEXT FEW days were a blur of family and friends in and out of the house. Davis had come out of surgery, and they thankfully were able to save his leg. The surgeons were able to use metal pins and plates to put his leg back together and, in their words, he was lucky to have survived the accident. He would require extensive physiotherapy to regain use of his leg and would have permanent nerve damage. The prognosis was that he would have a long road to recovery and that his military career was over. He would be granted a medical discharge immediately.

On Christmas Day, Marnie got a phone call from Davis telling her he would likely be discharged by New Year's. His voice sounded weak and tired, not the voice of the man she knew so well. Despite this, she was so grateful he was alive. Her Davis was coming home, this time for good.

It was a bitterly cold January morning when a military medical transport van pulled into the driveway. Over the past week, family and friends had stepped up to help her prepare for this homecoming, making the house wheelchair accessible and bringing in a bed that would make it easier for him to get in and out of.

Marnie stood nervously on the front porch, Bea flagging her. "Let's go help." Bea said, patting her on the back and giving her a resigned look.

They came down the ramp and were greeted by two service men both in their army fatigues. One soldier opened the side of the van and Davis's handsome face came into view. Marnie wanted to jump inside the van, to grab him and wrap herself around him, but when she took in his flat green eyes and the grim line of his mouth, she took a step back. The man she loved so much was broken, both in body and spirit. They strapped his wheelchair to the lift in the vehicle and slowly lowered him to the ground. His leg was cast from just above the knee and braced in front of him on a stabilizing footrest. She watched as they unstrapped him and rolled him towards the walkway.

"We'll help you get him inside." One soldier offered as he pushed him up the ramp towards the front door. Marnie opened the door and watched as they brought him inside and Bea thanked them, saying they had it from here. The men nodded and left, leaving them alone with Davis. No words had yet been spoken between them. Davis's head hung low, not making eye contact.

"Davis, we're so happy you're home." Bea said, wrapping her arms around him carefully.

Davis glanced up at Marnie and she crouched down, keeping her eyes locked with his. "Hi, baby," she said simply. "I love you."

He didn't respond at first, just stared at her blankly, until he reached for her hand, gripping it tightly. "I love you too, Sugar."

Marnie's body exhaled as she gingerly hugged him, his arms coming around her in a warm embrace. *My husband is finally home.* A sense of relief leaving her body but a huge weight of responsibility on her heart.

THE MONTH of January went by quickly and a routine had been forged. Bea had arranged for home care to come in and help with Davis's care while Marnie was at work. Marnie relied on family and her employees more now, with her working skeleton hours, so she could be with Davis as much as possible. He spent most of his time in bed, sleeping long hours and seldom would come into the kitchen or living room. Marnie set herself up with a cot next to his bed so she could be there at night if he needed her, opting not to sleep next to him with fear of hurting him inadvertently in his sleep. Many nights he would wake her, groaning and cursing from the pain in his sleep. Many nights she sat up and simply watching him. As she stared at him, a man so big and strong, looking so helpless in the bed, emotion would overflow as she let the tears fall. Tonight was one such night, and she held her head in her hands as she cried softly.

"Sugar?" Davis's deep voice cut through the darkness. She looked up, his head turned to face her. "Are you crying?"

She let out a long-pained exhale before she answered solemnly. "Yes."

"Come lie down with me," he requested, shifting his body and patting the space next to him.

She stood, rounded the foot of the bed, and carefully climbed in. He turned his face and reached over, running his large hand over her cheek in a sweet caress. She could make out the green of his eyes and furrowed brows in the dim light coming from the window.

"Don't cry, Marnie. I'm here and I'll be okay."

She lifted herself and brushed her lips to his, Davis responding in a tender embrace. The feel of his lips bringing emotion to the surface again. She broke their kiss and swallowed down the painful lump that constricted her throat.

"I need to feel you next to me," he said, pulling her towards him, her head resting on his chest. Arm wrapping around her, he placed a kiss on her head, the warmth of his body a soothing balm to her soul as they fell asleep.

* * *

SEVERAL MONTHS PASSED, the last of the winter snow melting as signs of spring popped up around Primrose. Davis hadn't left the house once, but today would be his first outing. He was still wheelchair bound, but after today he may be given the option of crutches, and the idea of being upright was something he had been looking forward to.

The past few months had been agonizing. The pain, the mental toll of the entire accident and the fact that he was unable to love his beautiful wife the way he wanted were all things that ate at him daily. Even with all this, he was so happy to be alive. The day of the accident played back in his mind like a slow-motion movie, going through each part, analyzing what went wrong. His last memory being knocked to the ground and the deafening sound of bone crushing followed by excruciating pain. When he was told the details of the accident, he was indeed so lucky to be alive and that he still had his leg.

"Are you ready to get this cast off?" Bea asked as she rolled his wheelchair down the corridor of the hospital. Marnie was walking beside him, holding his hand, looking gorgeous in a red blouse, tight jeans that hugged her behind just right, and a black jacket. When he saw her in the morning, all the blood rushed south, and his pulse spiked. His wife was sexy, and he was grateful that his libido was still very much alive and well.

"I'm very ready, but a little nervous about what it looks like underneath. They had to piece me back together a bit so it may not be pretty," he replied, furrowing his brows.

"Battle scars. All superheroes have them." Bea added, giving Marnie a wink.

"I personally think it will just add to your hotness," Marnie deadpanned.

"Oh, really?" Davis laughed and as she offered him a sexy grin and squeezed his hand.

An hour later Davis's cast was removed and the extent of what his leg had been through was very evident by the series of large scars, starting at his knee and going to the base of his calf, both from incisions and from the accident itself. His breath caught in his throat when he saw it as Bea and Marnie looked at him with compassion in their eyes. Davis had never been a vain man, but he had to admit it was painful to look at.

Noticing his shock, Marnie squeezed his hand and said, "Remember, you are here."

He nodded, knowing she was right. He was lucky to be alive, and he needed to focus on that.

After his cast was removed, and an air boot was fitted. His doctor walked him through a mobility recovery plan, which would include extensive physiotherapy. Even with a game plan in place, his doctor made it clear that he would likely never be able to run again and would have permanent nerve damage. Hearing this news was difficult, but there was only one thing he was concerned about at the moment.

"I have one more question," he asked the doctor as he

glanced at Marnie, a twinkle in his eye. "When can we commence bedroom activities?"

His doctor let out a chuckle, and Davis noticed a rosy hue swell on Marnie's face. "As long as things are working the way they should, and you're careful with your leg, you can have sex. Just nothing too vigorous, though."

Davis turned and waggled his eyebrows at Marnie, who was now as red as her shirt as the doctor simply laughed and sent them on their way.

* * *

"I STILL CAN'T BELIEVE you asked the doctor that." Marnie commented as she pulled out pajamas and set them on the bed.

Davis was given the option of crutches and had already become very adept at getting around with them. She watched as he sat down and pulled his shirt off. The sight of his muscular upper body making her tamped down desire rise to the surface.

"Can you help me with my pants?" he asked, rising from the bed, balanced on his crutches, and facing her. Seductively sauntering over to him, she stopped in front of him, staring up through her long lashes.

"Do you want to sleep naked?" she asked, teasing the waistband of his sweatpants and slowly sliding them over his hips and behind. His breath hitched, and a low, deep growl rumbled from his chest. "Marnie. I want you so much."

She gave him a coquettish grin as she knelt, helping him carefully step out of his pants, her eyes never leaving his. Rising to her feet, she curled her fingers in the waist-band of his boxer briefs, then started sliding them down too. It had been over a year and a half since they had been intimate, and seeing him hard and ready for her made her core ache for him to be inside her.

Davis seated himself on the bed and put his hands on her hips, looking up at her. She slowly unbuttoned her blouse, his eyes watching as with each button more and more of her skin was exposed. His eyes roamed her breasts as his hands slid up her stomach to cup the underside. She reached behind her back, unfastening her bra, and slipped out of it, leaving her bare in front of him. His eyes met hers so much love and sincerity in his gaze.

"You are so beautiful, Marnie. Just so fucking beautiful."

With a smile, she leaned down and kissed him softly, reverently, but when his tongue traced the line of her lips, she opened to him, allowing their kiss to deepen as their tongues tangled. He reached for the button of her jeans, popping it, and sliding them over her hips and behind, then down her legs. She stepped away to remove them and slid her panties down, leaving her completely exposed.

"I don't want to hurt you." She confessed, as he beckoned her to stand in front of him with his lustful eyes.

"I'll tell you if it's too much." He said as he shimmied himself to the middle of the bed, propped against pillows cushioning the headboard. She climbed over his lap, her core directly over his hard ridge. "Let's go slow," he suggested.

She positioned herself as he guided himself into her body, inch by glorious inch until he was fully buried in her warmth.

He reached up, cupping her face in his hands, his eyes hazy with lust as he kissed her deeply, all the pain of the past few months washing away in that moment as they moved in tandem, making love slowly and reverently.

As Davis and Marnie rediscovered each other in every way they possibly could, spending as much time together as they could to strengthen their relationship, Davis started the long road to recovery from his injuries. With intense physiotherapy, having to learn to walk on and trust his leg again, the progress was slow, painful, and excruciating to watch. His demanding therapy trickled into the days afterwards, causing Davis to escape the pain with sleep to help him deal with it. One thing Marnie noticed was Davis was emphatically against taking any strong pain relief. When she asked, he would say he had seen addiction before and was not about to follow down the same path as his mother. Knowing his childhood, she respected his stance.

In April they got amazing news that Garrett and Bea were expecting a baby in September. Both were beyond excited for them, and their news brought the prospect of a family back into their thoughts and conversation.

"How many kids do you want?" Marnie asked as she

peeked into a pot she had cooking on the stove. The smell of chilis and spices tickled Davis's senses as his stomach rumbled.

"A house full," he replied with a broad smile.

She rolled her eyes at him and laughed. "Let's start with one and go from there," she replied, giving him a wink.

"Does this mean you're ready to start trying?" he asked, watching intently for her reaction to his question.

She sauntered around the peninsula slowly, seductively, swaying her hips, his eyes watching every sashay. She straddled his hips where he sat on a kitchen chair and embraced him passionately, his desire awakening with their kiss as she whispered her reply against his lips, "I'm ready."

He kissed her again and met her gaze. "Now I have to figure out the job situation."

Marnie got off his lap and made her way back into the kitchen as she asked, "What are your options?"

"With my mechanical engineering degree, ideally working for a construction company," he replied. "I was talking to Hayden about it the other day and he said there's a new construction company that opened recently in Primrose, right next to the hardware store. Jaxon Isley owns it and is doing the renovations at Hayden's house right now."

"Well, that sounds promising." Marnie added. "Why don't you pop in there one day and talk to him? Do you know Jaxon?"

"A little. He was in school with Hayden, so I remember him vaguely. The Isley family is super well known in this area, though. His father was the mayor for many years."

"I would talk to him. How perfect would that be? Plus, then, you would be just down the street from me," she added with a bright smile.

Davis thought about that, and how using his degree and military experience would be an asset to Jaxon's business. He knew what he had to do to impress Jaxon and have him offer him a job. Looking at Marnie, a sense of contentment washed over him, knowing they now had a game plan for their future.

* * *

DAVIS HOBBLED up to the door of Isley Construction and took a deep breath. After his conversation with Marnie, he spoke to Hayden again, and he, too, encouraged him to go in to see Jaxon. Having made an appointment with him, he was eager to find out the possibilities.

"Davis!" Jaxon greeted, coming out of the office as he entered the building. Jaxon Isley, a former professional baseball player, was tall, athletic in build and had longish hair that curled at the ends and dark facial scruff. Not having seen him in years, it was only when he smiled Davis recognized him.

Balancing on his crutches, Davis extended his hand to give him a shake. "Hello Jaxon, nice to officially meet you."

"Yes, I remember you though, not hard to forget the red hair of a Baxter." he said teasingly, clapping him on the shoulder.

"It is our calling card," Davis agreed with a chuckle.

Jaxon led him into his office and gestured for him to take a seat. Davis obliged and leaned in, handing him a resume. Jaxon looked it over, his eyes widening, and he smiled, setting it down on the desk. "I appreciate you preparing this for me, but Davis, I don't need it."

Davis's heart sank as he met Jaxon's gaze. *Quick and painless. Alright then.*

"Davis, I would like to offer you a job. Hayden told me all about you, what you've been through, and all about your Mechanical Engineering Degree and experience through the military." He informed, leaning back in his seat with a smile. "Firstly, thank you for your service," he said with a respectful nod. "You served a long time and I myself am grateful to you for that." A deep swell of pride formed in his chest from Jaxon's kind words and Davis nodded, accepting the thanks. "And secondly, you would be a huge asset to Isley Construction. I have lots of projects lined up, in particular a condo complex and townhomes going up on the west side of town. Having someone like you with your expertise with regards to the structure and design of these buildings will help me create safe living spaces for individuals and families."

"Sounds exciting. I would love to be a part of your upcoming projects." Davis replied earnestly. "That is exactly the kind of work I was hoping to do."

For the next hour, the men talked in detail about the job description, salary, and when he would start. The project would break ground in one month, and Jaxon needed him to start as soon as possible. He also was flexible with the hours, allowing Davis to attend any therapy and medical appointments he had scheduled and work from home if he needed. Davis came away from their meeting feeling a sense of accomplishment that he had never experienced before. This would be his first job out of the military, and he was excited to get started.

As he left Isley Construction, he glanced down the main street towards Marnie's bakery just a block down. He couldn't wait to tell her and the walk, or in his case, hobble to the bakery wasn't far. He made his way down the sidewalk, passing residents all graciously allowing him to pass and offering him their hellos and smiles. The simple kindness of Primrose reminded him why he loved his hometown.

When he arrived at the bakery, a couple exiting held the door open for him so he could enter the building. The smell of coffee and delicious baked goods filled the air around him. In particular, the sweet smell of cinnamon, sugar, and savory butter. *Cinnamon Bun Day. Could this day get any better?*

"Davis!" Bea's voice sounded as he glanced to the side to find his sister at a table with her friends, Whitney and Ever Hastings.

He smiled as she gestured him over and he made his way to their table in the corner.

"Will you join us?" Ever asked as Bea moved a free chair over for him to sit at the end of the table, giving him more room for his crutches.

"Sure. I would love to," he said with an appreciative smile. "I need a bit of a rest," he said, setting his crutches against the wall and letting out a long breath.

"Where were you coming from?" Bea asked. "I know you can't drive yet."

"I was just at Isley Construction. I met with Jaxon this morning and he…"

Marnie's melodic voice interrupted his sentence. "Fresh cinnamon buns, right out of the oven, ladies!" she announced as she came around the corner of the counter and stopped seeing Davis. Her brows furrowed as she frowned. "Baby, you were supposed to call me when you were done. How did you get here?" she asked, looking him over.

"I managed; it wasn't too far," he said, gesturing to his crutches. "Besides, I couldn't wait to share the news." Marnie set the tray of cinnamon buns on the counter and looked at him curiously, a smile curving her lips. "Jaxon offered me a job. He said he has some new developments breaking ground soon, and he needs my expertise."

Marnie squealed and sat down on his lap, wrapping her arms around him. "Baby, that's amazing! When do you start?"

"Next week." he replied proudly before she planted a chaste kiss on his lips.

Bea gave him a punch in the shoulder and Ever and Whitney cheered their congratulations. "I think we need to celebrate with cinnamon buns and coffee!" Bea exclaimed. "Or tea for Whitney and I." she added as they patted their collective baby bumps.

Davis looked at his sister and her friend and then up to Marnie, her eyes twinkling with happiness. Feeling unmeasurably blessed in that moment, he put his hand on her stomach, hoping that one day she would be pregnant with their child. He had a beautiful wife, a great new job and, God willing, he would have the family he had always dreamt of.

CHAPTER 19

With their 3rd anniversary fast approaching and their first one spent together, Marnie wanted to do something special for Davis. A little getaway, just the two of them. When Marnie thought about where she wanted to go, there was only one place that came to mind. A place she had been before and was itching to go again. A place that she wanted to share with Davis, her parents' home city of Merida, Mexico.

"Tell me more about where we are going exactly?" Davis asked as he placed some shirts into a suitcase.

"Merida. It's on the Yucatan Peninsula." Marnie replied, sitting on the bed. "It's incredibly beautiful. Its history goes back to the Mayans. I just know you are going to love it."

"And you've been there before?" he asked, sitting next to her.

"Yes, several times. My uncle owns a hacienda downtown. We're going to stay there and explore the city."

"Will we be going to a beach?"

"If you want, yes. Are you just trying to get me into a bikini?" she asked, raising her eyebrow at him.

"A man can try, can't he?" he asked playfully, kissing her shoulder.

Marnie giggled, pushed him away playfully and walked over to her dresser, digging through a drawer to produce a blue bikini.

Davis whistled and waggled his eyebrows at her. "Now that's what I am talking about."

* * *

DAVIS WAS LITERALLY VIBRATING with nervous excitement. He had never taken a trip simply for pleasure, let alone with his beautiful wife. With physiotherapy going well, his air boot had been removed, and he was now able to walk without crutches. He was thrilled to be free to move as he chose. With nerve damage causing lack of feeling in his leg, he did have issues with his balance, so he started using a cane, which Bea joked just added to his superhero character persona. Davis always loved how his sister made even the most difficult situation, light, and fun.

Determined to enjoy every moment with Marnie, they arrived at the small airport in Merida and slowly navigated through to luggage claim. Since they weren't going during the peak of the tourist season, they didn't have the challenge of large crowds to contend with. Running on pure adrenaline, Davis's body was tired and leg stiff from the flight, but he wasn't going to let that hinder him. They caught a shuttle to their destination and during the drive Davis marveled at the colorful old buildings, open restaurants, and beautiful historic buildings as he looked out the window.

"It's beautiful, isn't it?" Marnie asked.

Davis nodded and reached for her hand as he replied, "It's amazing your family is from here."

"Yes, I still have a few relatives here. Mostly distant, but my uncle and a few cousins still reside in and around Merida. I've only been here a few times, but have some of my best memories here."

Arriving at their destination, the midafternoon sun was high as the shuttle stopped in front of the Hacienda de la Rosa in downtown Merida. From the outside it was a brightly painted terracotta color stucco building that looked very plain and unassuming. However, when they walked inside a large bright foyer greeted them with tall ceilings, colorful artwork, and rich dark leather furniture, that simply invited you to sit down and relax.

A man in his late 50s with salt and pepper hair and matching moustache was at the front desk and looked up from his computer, a huge smile and look of recognition on his face. He rounded the front desk while putting out his arms in greeting. "Martina?" he asked. "Eres tu?"

"Hola Tío! Coma estas?" she asked, giving him a big hug.

"Good, good! Oh, my goodness, you have grown into such a beautiful young woman!" he said, taking her hands and holding her out at arm's length to look her over. "I haven't seen you in at least 10 years. I'm sorry I couldn't come to your wedding."

Marnie waved off his apology. "That's okay Tio, we were married so quickly with little time to plan, so I didn't expect you to be there. Tio, I would like to introduce you to my husband Davis Baxter." she said, gesturing to Davis.

Davis took him in, seeing the family resemblance immediately, and put his hand out to her uncle in greeting. "Nice to meet you, sir."

He laughed a rich, bountiful laugh that shook his entire body and exclaimed, "Oh, call me Tio!" He let his eyes drift down to Davis's cane and his scarred leg. "I heard you were injured recently and were in the military?"

"Yes. I served 14 years."

"I want to hear all about it, and I'm sure you have many stories to tell, but for now let's get you two lovers into a room so you can rest from your travels." he said gesturing for them to join him at the front desk. He checked them in and walked them to their room at the end of the large, lush garden in the center of the Hacienda. The smell of fragrant gardenia bushes permeated the space, and the vibrant green lawn was nicely manicured. At one end of the garden area was a small pool and lounging chairs, perfect for a lazy afternoon under the Mexican sun.

Stopping at large ornate doors, he turned to them and unlocked the door. "This is the honeymoon suite and our largest room we have available," he said, bringing them into the large bedroom and holding his arms out. "I hope it is to your liking."

Davis walked in and was greeted by a beautiful bright room, with rich yellow on the walls, a cozy seating area with dark leather furniture and a large dark wood four-poster king size bed. Deep sapphire blue linens, large colorful pillows dressed the bed and light gauzy material was draped over each corner cascading down the posters. To one side of the bed was a large dark wood armoire and dresser, and off the main space was a large bathroom with a colorful tiled corner shower and large vanity. Everything about the room felt welcoming and relaxing.

"Tio, this is perfect." Marnie said, looking around. "Thank you."

"Anything for my hermosa Martina." he said, placing the key in her hand and planting a kiss on her cheek. "Davis, I look forward to getting to know you better," he said, shaking his hand. "Perhaps if you don't have plans, you two can join me for dinner later tonight in my apartment? Say at 7 p.m.?"

"That sounds great." Davis replied, looking at Marnie for confirmation as she nodded and smiled at Tio in agreement.

"Okay, now rest. Hasta luego."

The door to their room closed and Davis looked around again and over at Marnie. "This is beyond amazing," he said, approaching her. He stumbled in his approach and Marnie's brows furrowed in concern.

"I think you need some rest before we explore. It has been a long day on your feet," she said, wrapping her arms around him and giving him a chaste kiss. "Do you want to take a nap with me?"

He nodded and made his way to the bed, set his cane aside where it was reachable and flopped down on the bed, pillows propped behind him. As he sat there, he watched Marnie move around the room, unpacking their suitcases. When she was done, she slowly started to strip out of her clothes, knowing he was watching. "Is this a naked nap?" he asked coyly, watching her undress.

"It is. I plan on being naked as much as possible on this trip." she said, crawling onto the bed seductively and reaching for his belt buckle.

He watched her strip him piece by piece and when they were both naked, laying together, their bodies inter-twined, he mused, "I think I'm going to like Mexico."

* * *

AFTER A LONG REFRESHING NAP, they showered and got ready for an evening with Tio. Marnie, knowing the way, brought them to the private part of the Hacienda, which was her uncle's residence. Tio greeted them and invited them into his large apartment with an open kitchen and living area and hallway leading to bedrooms. It too, was bright and inviting like the rest of the hacienda. Off the living area was a veranda overlooking the street below where you could hear the chatter of pedestrians and open patios as well as the sound of traffic in the distance. When they entered the space, the delicious smell of slow cooked pork, spices and citrus greeted them.

"I hope you like Cochinita Pibil!" Tio exclaimed, lifting the lid of a pot, steam rising from the casserole.

Davis looked at Marnie for an explanation. "It's pork with lots of spices and sour orange that is slow cooked in a banana leaf."

"That sounds amazing!" Davis replied, inhaling the delicious aroma.

Tio gestured for them to have a seat at his round kitchen table and turned his gaze to Davis. "I want to hear all about your experiences in the military." So as Tio finished off their dinner of slow cooked pork, homemade tortillas, and pickled onions along with beans, rice and chicharron. They talked about Davis's military career and his accident, Tio asking questions with genuine curiosity. Tio sat back in his chair, shaking his head. "Well, young man, you have been through a lot."

Davis nodded in acknowledgment. "It wasn't easy, but honestly, the hardest part of it all was being away from Marnie," he said, reaching over to take her hand. Marnie gave him a loving smile and leaned in to brush her lips to his.

Tio looked between them, smiling with admiration. "My sister, Martina's Madre, has told me about your relationship, the loss, the hardship being apart, and she has also told me how deeply in love you are with each other. Now seeing you two it makes my heart ache for my dear Lola."

Brows drawing together, Marnie offered Tio a sad look and turned to Davis, explaining. "Lola was my Tia. Tio's wife. She passed away from cancer 10 years ago. The last time we were here was for her funeral."

Davis turned to Tio, empathy in his eyes. "I'm sorry for your loss."

Tio smiled wistfully and bowed his head in thanks. "It was so long ago already, but losing her, my love, my friend, was so hard. And now when I see you, and from what I have been told of your story, it reminds me so much of our relationship." He looked off to the sky beyond the veranda, thinking about his next words before he continued. "Lola and I experienced great love, and great loss, too. While we now have four grown children, all with their own families, we lost a baby as well."

Marnie looked at her uncle, her eyes wide. "I didn't know that," she said, choking on her words.

"Oh, not too many people know. Your mother doesn't even know. We were young and not married yet. Just two loco kids in love when Lola found out she was pregnant. We were excited and planned to get married as soon as possible, but then she lost the baby, and we broke off our engagement." Davis's eyes met Marnie's as he squeezed her hand, and both looked back to Tio as he continued. "I loved her, and would not take no for an answer. I pursued her, and she finally agreed to marry me. We were still so much in love, and we had a happy marriage. 26 years together."

Marnie sat back and let out a long exhale. "Your story is so similar to ours."

Tio nodded and sat up straight, resting his arms on the table as he looked from Davis to Marnie. "Not every path to happily ever after is a straight line. Sometimes the path is curved or goes in a circle. Sometimes it's smooth and a lot of times it's rocky. Sometimes you are given obstacles so big you think you can never get over them. Sometimes you will want to give up and turn back. But if you love each other and you choose every day to walk together, I promise you will find all the happiness you seek and more. That is what Lola and I found, and I can see that is what you have found together."

Marnie's eyes stung with tears at her uncle's profound

words and her heart felt full. She glanced at Davis, her eyes meeting his, glistening with unshed tears. She caressed his cheek as she leaned in and kissed him tenderly. They had experienced a rocky path thus far in their short marriage, and although she was certain there would be challenges ahead. They were choosing to walk that path together.

That night, they lay in bed wrapped around each other, thinking about the wonderful evening they spent with Tio.

"Tio is such a wise man." Davis said with a reflective smile.

"He is. I never knew his love story with Tia until today. It was beautiful." Marnie echoed, resting her chin on his chest and meeting his eyes.

"And it wasn't perfect." Davis added. "But they overcame their obstacles together and had a truly happy life."

Marnie nodded and replied. "When I think of the journey you and I have been on, I don't think I would have changed anything. Honestly, it was difficult at the time, but I think we were meant to experience all the hardship and loss so we could appreciate all the good times ahead. So, we could appreciate each other more."

"So, we could appreciate all the sweetness this life has to offer," he added with a smile as he smoothed his fingers over the maple leaf pendant around her neck.

She nodded and winked at him. "Two prairie hearts."

"Two prairie hearts," he whispered.

Peeling herself from his side, she climbed onto his lap, straddling his hips, her eyes transfixed on his brilliant green eyes. "I love you, Davis. You have made my life so sweet, and I'm so happy and grateful I get to choose you every day."

He met her gaze, so much emotion in his eyes. "Thank you for loving me and never giving up on me. I love you, Sugar."

Their lips met in a tangle of emotion, passion, and undying love. A kiss to wash away all the past, hurt and pain. A kiss that planted a promise of a beautiful future together. As they kissed, their thirst for each other grew, needing to be quenched. No words needing to be said, both knowing what each other needed. They connected, their bodies joining in sweet pleasure. They made love, slowly, reverently. Their intense connection, hungry and ravenous. As the wave of their desire crested and they crashed to the shore together, they both knew that now and for the rest of their lives, they were one.

The next week in Merida was magical and more than either could have asked for. They spent their days exploring the sites, like the landmark of Paseo de Motejo, the beautiful Cathedral de Merida and the Mayapan Archaeological Zone. They dined on the most delicious food at quaint restaurants, spending hours sitting on their outdoor patios eating, drinking, laughing, talking, and doing a lot of kissing. They spent time lazing on the beach or by the pool at the hacienda soaking up the hot Mexican sun. They shopped at adorable little shops and took in the vibrant music and culture. They made love any chance they could and, if it was possible, they fell deeper in love with each other. This trip, a catalyst to heal their souls.

* * *

UPON THEIR RETURN from their euphoric vacation, summer was in full swing in Primrose. Everyone was outside walking main street, visiting neighbors, the smell of fresh cut grass and barbeques wafting through the air. Not having seen too many friends since their trip to Merida, Ben and Ever invited all their friends over for a barbeque at Prairie Sky and some summer fun. The mid-July heat was in full force, and everyone found themselves gathered under the shade of the porch with plates of food and drinks in hand.

"Davis, I have to say you're getting around pretty good these days." Hayden commented, watching him balance a plate of food while walking with his cane.

"Yep, almost ready to kick this thing to the curb," he said, holding up his cane. "I'm starting to get some feeling back in my leg, so that's good. The hardest part has been learning to trust my leg again. It's hard to trust something is going to hold you up when you can't feel it."

"Well, you have come so far!" Ever exclaimed. "Hey how was Mexico?"

Davis and Marnie looked at each other with a dreamy look in their eyes.

Bea climbed the porch stairs, with her baby belly perfectly round like she swallowed a basketball, a Wonder Woman t-shirt not quite covering her burgeoning belly. She stopped in front of them, put her hands on her hips and said, "That look means you two never left the bedroom, doesn't it?"

Marnie shrugged and volleyed back, "Isn't that what a honeymoon is for?"

"Touche." she replied, curling up on Garrett's lap as he fed her potato chips.

Everyone laughed and Whitney replied with a slight pout, "Hayden and I never got a honeymoon."

Hayden put his hand on Whitney's huge baby belly, their 4th, a little girl on the way in August. "That's because we keep getting pregnant," he said with a sweet smile. "But I promise after these renovations are done, I will have your parents come out, take care of the kids and we will go on vacation, wherever you want, gorgeous." She gave him a big grin and planted a long, lingering kiss on his lips.

"Get a room!" Bea yelled across the porch, rolling her eyes as she grabbed another chip from Garrett's fingers with her teeth, making everyone laugh.

Amelia came running onto the porch with Ever and Ben's six-year-old twin girls, Violet and Poppy, the three Hastings boys, Bauer, Beckett and Bodhi following close behind and one-year-old Luke on her hip.

"Can we have Popsicles?" Amelia asked on behalf of her crew of kids. All the kids nodding, big sweaty dirty smiles on their faces from playing outside in the July heat.

"You sure can." Ever replied. "They're in the freezer. Are you able to help everyone, Amelia?"

She nodded as all the kids followed her through the front door, the storm door slamming behind them. Everyone looked at Bea and Garrett.

"Now that is a great kid. Big sister extraordinaire right there," Hayden complimented.

Bea smoothed her hand down at her baby bump and smiled at Garrett, pride and love radiating between them.

Marnie looked between her friends, taking in each couple, so much in love surrounding each of them. Each one living life to the fullest and standing by each other through all of life's challenges. Each couple had their own story, their own highs, their own lows, but they stuck it out. She looked at Davis, who met her eyes, giving her a knowing look that he felt it too. Snuggling into her husband, he wrapped his arm around her, pulling her close, both enveloped with the blissful feeling of being truly blessed.

* * *

TWO WEEKS LATER, on a very hot July day, Bea gave birth to a beautiful little girl, who they named Ruby. She arrived five weeks early, and although she was small, she was simply perfect.

Marnie cradled Ruby in her arms, her sweet face, rosy cupid's bow lips and button nose so adorable it made her heart swell. Davis looked at Marnie, their eyes meeting as she cuddled the little bundle. A knowing glance passed between them, saying that this was what they wanted. "Would you like to hold her?" Marnie asked, taking one last smell of her sweet head.

Davis smiled, put his arms out, and Marnie passed the newborn baby to him. He cuddled his new niece, a wide smile painted across his face.

"Looking good there, Davis." Bea commented, coming around the kitchen island and bringing them each a cup of coffee.

"She's beautiful Bea." he said, looking up, his eyes glossed over with emotion.

"Yeah, we made a pretty cute kid," Bea replied, reaching for Garrett's hand and giving it a squeeze.

He smiled at his wife and deadpanned. "I am destined to be around gingers."

Everyone laughed and Marnie looked down at the beautiful red curls on Ruby's head. *Would their child have that signature Baxter trait?* She rested her hand on her belly. In eight months, they would find out.

* * *

MARNIE ENTERED the Tattoo studio in St. Augustine and glanced around, looking for Davis, who she spotted at a cubicle in the back corner. She was greeted by a woman at the front counter who had a brightly colored sleeve on full display. "I'm looking for my husband. He is right back there," she said, pointing towards the back corner.

"Go ahead." She gestured with a kind smile.

Marnie made her way past cubicles and big tattooed men, all friendly, offering her a lingering look and a smile. She reached Davis, his scarred leg propped up and the tattoo artist hard at work. Marnie's eyes widened as she took in his new ink, still in progress. Over his scars two maple leaves were inked, in rich bright colors, merging a design of gardenias and daisies, and the artist was now incorporating one tiny shamrock into the design.

Davis smiled at her sweetly. "The maple leaves are for us; the flowers are for you and the shamrock is for DJ." he shared.

"It's beautiful." She replied, taking in the design. "But it's missing something."

Davis's brows knit together. He glanced down at his leg and up to Marnie, meeting her gaze. The tattoo artist stopped and looked up at her as well.

"You are going to have to add another shamrock." She replied with a coy smile.

Davis was silent for a moment as realization dawned, and his eyes widened in question. "Are you pregnant?"

"I am 12 weeks along today and everything is healthy," she replied, pulling a sonogram photo out of her purse and handing it to him.

Davis took the photo and looked up at her, his brilliant green eyes shining with tears as he whispered. "Our baby."

She nodded and let out a sing-song giggle. Davis shifted in the seat and reached for her, bringing her onto his lap. The tattoo artist rose from his stool, gave them a knowing smile and excused himself, leaving them alone for a moment.

"We're having a baby," Davis whispered, a tear rolling down his cheek.

"We're having a baby," she confirmed, leaning in to capture the tear with a kiss. She looked into the eyes of the man she loved more than life itself and brought her lips to his, a kiss full of tenderness, desire and promise for a lifetime of love ahead.

EPILOGUE

5 years later

Marnie closed her eyes, taking in the feel of the light Fall breeze on her face. There wasn't a cloud in the sky, and the sun was unseasonably warm for early October. It was Thanksgiving weekend and tomorrow both she and Davis would have to return to their weekly routine, her at the bakery and him on the construction site. She opened her eyes and turned, smoothing her hand over the plaque on the bench she was seated on. "For DJ." The plaque simply read. She thought of the baby they lost so many years ago. This bench, a reminder that he was a part of their story.

Breaking her out of her melancholy, she heard the sweet giggles of her daughter and the deep, rich laughter of her husband. She turned to watch as Davis slid down the slide of the elementary school play structure with their two-year-old daughter, Lola, on his lap. Her wild, curly, dark brown hair and brilliant green eyes twinkling, her cheeks rosy and her squeal of delight drifting on the breeze. Every time she saw Davis with their children, she was reminded of how incredibly blessed they were. He was a loving and attentive father, and it warmed her heart every day.

"Mama!" the voice of their four-year-old son, Finn, sounded as she turned to see him running from the line of trees that framed the schoolyard where he liked to explore and play. "Mama, look what I found," he said excitedly.

"What do you have there, Finny?" she asked as he reached her, his round face speckled with dirt, his chocolate brown eyes glinting with his discovery. "I found these," he said, holding out a bunch of colorful leaves he had gathered from the trees.

"Oh, let's see," Marnie replied, putting out her hand for him to show her. She took in the collection he had gathered; leaves of every color, and she held each one up for him to tell her the color he saw. Finn was going to start kindergarten next year, loved to learn, and knew all his primary colors. Marnie glanced at the last one in her hand—a maple leaf. She reached up and touched the pendant around her neck, a smile curving her lips.

"That one is red!" Finn exclaimed proudly.

Marnie nodded and tousled her son's dark brown hair. "Yes, baby, it is. Do you know what kind of leaf this is?" she asked, her eyebrow raised in question. He shook his head, his beautiful brown eyes curious as she answered. "This is a maple leaf, from a maple tree," she explained.

"Like maple syrup?" Finn asked brightly.

"Yes, baby, maple syrup comes from maple trees." She answered. "This leaf is extra special too because whenever you see one you can pick it up and know that you are loved."

Finn took the leaf from her and smoothed his chubby little hand over the lines and ridges, taking in the details. He handed it back to Marnie and leaned in to give her a kiss on the cheek. "I love you, mama," he said, wrapping his arms around her neck in a hug. She held him tightly, feeling her heart burst at his sweet declaration. Letting him go, he ran towards the play structure but suddenly turned around, flashing her his sweet smile. "Can we have pancakes for dinner tonight?"

Marnie giggled and nodded. "Yes, Finny."

"Did I hear pancakes?" Davis asked as he made his way towards her and tousled Finn's hair, making him giggle.

Marnie admired her husband as he slowly sauntered up to her with his red hair now longer and curling out at the ends, the trim red beard he now sported, that she found incredibly sexy. Although he was still bulky, muscular, and burly, he now had more of a dad bod, and honestly Marnie found that incredibly sexy too. She took in the gait of his walk and the slight limp he now had, the daily reminder of what he had been through so many years ago. All these simple imperfections, making him more attractive in her eyes. Five years later, she still thought he was the hottest man she had ever seen and, as promised in her vows, she told him and showed him every day. "Hey there, hot stuff." Marnie said flirtatiously, giving him a sexy grin.

"Hey there, Sugar." he replied, sliding in next to her on the bench. He glanced down at the maple leaf she was still holding and looked up, meeting her eyes. So much love, happiness, and contentment in his gaze. "Two prairie hearts," he whispered, leaning in and gently brushing his lips to hers. "Two prairie hearts." Marnie echoed, lacing her hand with his as she rested her head on his shoulder, and they watched their children play.

* * *

Thank you for reading Prairie Hearts!
Want more steamy romance set in the idyllic small town
of Primrose?
Read Prairie Sound now!

ALSO BY TANYA RENEE

Primrose Series
Prairie Sky

Prairie Nights

Prairie Fire

Prairie Hearts

Prairie Sound

The Spring of Love Series

By Virginia Taylor

Forever Delighted

Forever Amused

Forever Heartfelt

The Tooth Fairy Chronicles

By Victoria Rocus

Tooth Decay With A Side Of Fae

Toothaches And Wedding Cakes

Baby Tooth And Tangled Roots

Wisdom Tooth And The Awful Truth

A New Page

by Aimee MacRae

It Happened in Paris

By Michelle Beesley

For more information visit:

www.serenadepublishing.com

ABOUT THE AUTHOR

Tanya Renee is a proud Canadian Prairie girl, who grew up on a family farm in Southeastern Manitoba Canada. Always an avid reader, she became intrigued with the romance genre at an early age when she first read Romeo and Juliet. Soon after she started to craft her own stories and poetry and by the time she was in high school, she had declared someday she would become a writer.

Married to the love of her life, she resides in Steinbach, Manitoba Canada with two teenagers and a menagerie of pets. When she's not cooking up a storm in her kitchen, she can be found tinkering in her garden, drinking copious amounts of coffee with a book in hand, listening to 80's music/audio books or at her laptop creating stories that are emotionally satisfying. She writes what she wants to read, epic stories that bring you on a journey and make you believe in love.

www.tanyareneeromance.com

ACKNOWLEDGMENTS

I want to start by thanking all of those that choose to serve our country. Your dedication to serving and protecting astounds me and I am grateful for your sacrifice. To the military families who hold it together at home, plain and simple, you truly are superheroes. My gratitude and respect to both.

To my husband, Bart, my rock, my confidante, my sounding board. Your unfailing belief in me is like fuel to my writing. I love you.

To my kids, Theo and Raina, who willingly listen to their mom prat on about my characters and book ideas and get excited when my books chart on Amazon. You two are the best and my greatest accomplishment in life is being your mom! I love you, kiddos!

To my mom and dad, who have instilled a work ethic in me that I've carried through in all of life's adventures. Thank you for teaching me that with hard work anything is possible. Love you.

To my niece, Caitlin who I roughly based Marnie on. When I considered some of the qualities, I wanted Marnie to possess, independent, resilient, work ethic and an incredible entrepreneurial spirit, I immediately thought of you. Oh, and thank you for taking my first photos as a writer! You, as always, are awesome!

Thank you to the communities of Landmark, Manitoba, the inspiration for Primrose and Steinbach, Manitoba, the inspiration for St. Augustine. The support these communities have given me has been incredible and I am grateful to be a part of them.

Thank you to my readers, and to those that have fallen in love with Primrose and my cast of characters. Knowing my stories have in some way touched your heart or helped you through something, is all the validation I need to keep writing! You guys rock!

And lastly to my publisher, Sarah Williams, CEO of Serenade Publishing. Thank you for believing in me. Words cannot express how grateful I am to have you on my journey.

www.ingramcontent.com/pod-product-compliance
Lightning Source LLC
Chambersburg PA
CBHW030821210726
48290CB00002B/696